UNFORGIVABLE

FRANCIS H. POWELL

ISBN: 978-1-916551-05-3

THE MODERN DAY KILLER

CHAPTER 1

An Accidental Beginning

Hello, I am the notorious priest killer. Me, Mr Respectable. Michael Dawkins, aged forty-five, a man of no great significance.

What you are about to read may sound like the mad ramblings of a crazy person, and I couldn't blame you for thinking so. Yes, I am the one everyone has been talking about for quite some years, the one the world knows as the 'priest killer'. I won't deny it. In fact, I am happy to let the world know. I have felt suffocated by my own secrets for too long.

Many newspaper columns have been filled about the priest killer, along with a number of assumptions about the killer's identity. In a way, I suppose I have enjoyed reading so many misguided notions about the infamous killer. I had to laugh when the police arrested and charged the wrong man. Under pressure to nail the killer, they picked on an oddball university lecturer, pinning the crimes on him, on the hearsay of people reporting on his anti-Catholic rhetoric.

I had never intended to be a killer. I even married a devout Catholic. I have never held any grudges against priests apart from having to listen to dreary sermons and singing along to lacklustre hymns when I chose to join my wife at Church every so often. In a way, I have always felt a bit of sympathy for priests. A lifetime of being denied sex, living alone, lonesome and drab evenings - which is why so many take to the bottle.

The first priest I killed was not a priest yet, but a young prelate. It was a Sunday afternoon. My wife was visiting a friend of hers and with little to do, I had decided I would take my dog Merlin for a walk along a coastal path.

Winter was setting in, the weather inclement and a storm brewing. Sensible types were sheltered in the warmth of their homes. I wrapped up warm and put on waterproof clothes in readiness for a sudden downpour. I never expected to meet anybody – it was that kind of day. When suddenly, about fifteen minutes into my walk, a male figure staring out to the sea appeared.

This stretch of the coast was well known for suicides, and I thought it would be a good idea to talk to this black-clad man. On closer inspection, he was a good-looking young man, tall and lean, with carefully cut hair and sparkling blue eyes.

"Not very nice weather, is it?" I called to him, without much enthusiasm.

"Not so great, in fact," he replied, and I noticed he had a foreign accent, eastern European maybe.

"Out for an afternoon walk," I said, feeling a bit awkward and unsure what to say next.

"You could say that" he replied, head bowed as if something serious was bothering him.

"Are you from around here?" I inquired, trying to get a bit of conversation out of him. But he appeared to be painfully shy.

"Not really, no. I am finishing my training."

"What kind of training would that be?" I demanded.

"I am going to be a priest," he said with muted enthusiasm.

"That's nice," I said, feeling rather foolish because I felt a more meaningful comment would have been in order.

"A lifetime serving God, I added, a lifetime of

devotion and sacrifice, what a virtuous thing to do."

"I am not sure," he replied solemnly.

"What do you mean?" I asked, by now full of curiosity.

"I have doubts, grave doubts. I feel like my whole life has been planned for me by my parents. I am the eldest son, you see, and they have always told me I should become a priest. Who am I to crush their dreams?"

Such a nice young man, I thought to myself, but so tormented.

"Let's walk for a while together," I suggested, and he seemed happy to accept my proposal. He talked a lot about his family. They had come from Poland not that long ago. As soon as he had left school, he had found himself training to be a priest.

But living in a new country had opened his eyes about the priesthood. He'd even met a young English girl at school, who had wanted an intimate relationship. She'd got a friend of hers to pass him a note suggesting they go out one evening to *get to know each other better*.

When he had run the idea by his parents, they had been scathing. They had said it would be *inappropriate for somebody about to become a servant of God.* He told me they were not totally endeared to their host country and were sceptical of the English youth, and particularly those young girls in short skirts who seemed to flaunt their attributes even during the throes of winter.

I liked this young man and fully understood his predicament. It was me, however, who changed the course of his life for ever. Looking down at the ground, I picked up a stick and threw it, not realising we were so close to the cliff edge and the wind would send it further.

My dog bounded after the stick. However, my ill-thought-out action put my dog in serious peril, as it was close to hurtling over the cliff. The young Pole, alive to danger, ran towards my dog in a noble bid to save it. He tripped on some barbed wire that had been knocked over by a previous storm. The barbed wire wrapped itself around the young man's ankles. The ground had been sodden for weeks after a lot of heavy rain and the fence came easily out of the ground. The priest-in-the-making's dash to save my dog, combined with a sudden burst of wind, led him to plunge over the cliff, his legs gripped by barbed wire. I listened to his screams of helplessness and agony.

I lay on my stomach and moved cautiously on all fours towards my dog, who I shouted at to stay put. I managed to save my dog, but as I did so I caught a brief glimpse of the young prelate, swinging helplessly, attached to the edge of the cliff only by the barbed wire that was tearing into his flesh. It would either be a long, slow agonizing death, or he would eventually plunge onto the rocks.

Most people's natural reaction would have been to try to save the prelate, or at least to call the emergency services. My dog was safe, while this man, a reluctant servant of God, was in the process of losing his life. I casually got up, ignoring the prelate's screams, and continued walking, surprised by my own callousness. After a while, his screams were replaced by the increasingly ferocious rattling of the wind. Then the rain came down again in a violent burst. I grabbed my dripping dog and ran back to my car.

When I got home, I found my wife glaring at me angrily.

"Going out in this kind of weather," she scorned, "you must be mad!"

I didn't respond, I just laughed to downplay the situation, and failed to mention what had occurred by the cliff edge. It was a good week or two before the young prelate's body was identified. He'd left his college seminary unauthorized, and had taken a train to the coast, so nobody could have guessed his whereabouts and the police had drawn blanks for a while.

Desperate appeals had been made by his heartbroken parents for someone to come forward, but no one had been able to help. I certainly wasn't going to come to their aid and had watched the whole drama unfold, relishing it as my very own little secret. My wife even remarked I seemed *happier than usual.*

Ok I hadn't pushed this man over the cliff, but in a way, I still was the one responsible for putting him out of his misery and the life he was about to embark on, which would have been stark and joyless.

Priest killer, that's what I am, I thought to myself, *not just Mr Ordinary from Mediocre Street, Suburbia.*

CHAPTER 2

My Anger Gets the Better of Me

After this first incident, it took me a few years to establish myself as a genuine, fully-fledged priest killer. The second time I was given a similar opportunity started in mundane surroundings, as I was sitting in a train carriage. There was a bunch of noisy clean cut choir boys and pubescent girls on their way to a church concert, and I was forced to suffer their infernal, sanctimonious *utterances.*

They were accompanied by a young priest, the choir master, whom they kept referring to as Father Jethro - they seemed to worship him, for that matter.

As time went on, the hyped-up, church-brainwashed teenagers really started to get under my skin. I suppose they imagined they could convert the whole world. That the whole world should have their beliefs and follow the path they were following.

The priest seemed to delight in their exuberance rather than being conscious of the effect they were having on passengers, such as myself. My anger directed itself towards the priest. I expressed my discomfort, saying the carriage was not just for them, that other passengers didn't need to be subjected to these imposing zealots. My complaints were brushed aside with contempt.

By listening in to a call he made with his phone yes, he had a smart *phone,* and he was also apparently on Facebook I discovered that he had *a meeting* with another priest. The priests would be preparing the church while the choir settled in their hotel before the concert. There was an arrogance this young priest carried, that really got to me.

I decided quite irrationally, I *would follow* him. The teenagers did some singing "spreading the word of god" a warm-up, in the station once we arrived, accompanied by two playing acoustic guitar, doubtlessly annoying countless commuters rushing for their evening trains. Father Jethro conducted them, and then he left unsuspectingly with me on his tail. The children were allowed some free time in a cafe.

The church was handily placed not so far from the station. I saw the priest walk inside.

I heard two voices, chatting happily with one another. I was now bound not to kill one priest but two. They didn't notice as I slipped inside. The church was dark and shadowy. I discreetly bolted the church doors, to make sure I wasn't disturbed. I looked around the church *and seized* upon the idea of *using one* of the candle holders on the *alter.* I picked it up and ran towards the two priests and swung the candlestick holder in the direction of the annoyingly assured priest that had annoyed me on the train. The weapon I had chosen did the job, it landed on his head, splintering it, discharging parts of brain, letting out *an excruciating sound,* that I can still hear, when I resurface the chilling memory.

A few more blows and the young man's head was distorted beyond recognition as well as blood trailing along the stone floor of the church. I observed the other priest slightly older than him seemingly rooted in fear, whimpering. He'd been preparing the church for what was surely going to be a rousing occasion, now he'd observed a brutal murder and there was so much carnage in evidence, bits of Father Jethro's blood and brain splattered about, even on his black vestments.

The other priest made a futile dash to the door. As his hand reached for the latch, I landed a blow on the back of his head, which burst open and blood and cerebral parts discharged around him, like a ripe melon being pulverized by a hammer. He slithered down the door onto the floor, leaving a trail of blood. One blow had been efficient and enough to see to his demise.

It all happened very quickly. It was like I was in a trance, some force pushing me to do this unspeakable act. The older priest, I had no grudge to bare against him, had a nice amicable face, that was before I had smashed it beyond recognition.

I dragged the older priest back to where the younger one was. I laid them out to make them look like they were touching hands, as if they were connecting. I went into the vestry, there I found the younger priest's coat, which exchanged for mine. My coat had quite a bit of blood splattered on it. Having taken all my possessions out of the pockets, and placed them in my newly acquired coat, I put my coat in a bag I discovered full of booklets, with the words of hymns that were... before my intervention, about to be sung. I covered the priests with the booklets, to leave some kind *of unfathomable message.*

I was ready to leave. The vestry led to a side door out into a small alleyway. There was a key left in the keyhole, which allowed me to leave the church locked. I locked the door in the same manner I would my own house, calmly, inconspicuously. I was sure nobody would have noticed me or even given me a second glance.

I dumped my blood splattered coat in a dustbin, a fair way from the church, as I headed home. I would tell my wife, there had been a terrible delay on the train, a common enough occurrence. She would have no cause to doubt my tardiness. On the train I found in a pocket of the coat that had belonged to the young priest, a scrawled note.

It said…

Be my friend on Facebook, but I am sure we can be much more than Facebook friends!

I remembered the young girls had been swarming around the young priest, in such a way, it was obvious *they idolised him* more than the god they professed to worship. I screwed up the note, opened the window and discreetly let it out the window. It fluttered away, while the train edged closer to my station.

Later that evening there was some "breaking news". The local newsreaders spoke with revulsion of "this terrible profanity in a church no less". The public in particular church goers, catholic as well all the other denominations, were horrified. The police were "perplexed". Expert criminal journalists equally at a loss to make sense of what had happened at the church of St Ethelred. Was it some kind of religious violence?

While watching the evening news, as was our way each evening, after dinner had been consumed, my wife was lost for words. Finally, she muttered some words about the "sheer evil of the perpetrator".

When I accompanied my wife to our weekly mass at St Cuthberts, the priest Father Mack, who obviously was reeling from shock, but had some more forthright words to say…

"The sinner who carried out this abomination, will burn in Hell's fires while the two priests, who have been slaughtered in Christ's name will be welcomed to Christ's table and reside in heaven for all eternity."

What Father Mack or indeed the rest of the

congregation didn't know, much to my pleasure was that the sinner who will be burning in Hell, was in fact right among them, namely me. I managed to contain my mirth. The story carried on for weeks. The choir was devastated, waling adolescents, were interviewed, asked about Father Jethro, the priest the idolized. Some said he would shortly be made a Saint. A new Facebook page was set up in memoriam of Father Jethro. The choir sang at his funeral mass, each with tears in their eyes.

CHAPTER 3

An opportune crime, too good to resist.

Back to my normal routine with the police still hunting for clues I found myself driving, one winter's evening, as the light was closing in. It was a minor road, and it was highly unlikely I would encounter anybody at this time. I was mistaken. Father Tom O'Flanagan, in his thirties, kind of progressive for a priest, who liked to ride his bicycle. He liked to be seen, as man of God, but also a man of the people. He preached ecology in his sermons. I did not know him well, but I did know the kind of man he was…The "green" priest…who wanted not only to save souls but also the planet.

I was deep in my own thoughts when my eyes latched onto Father Tom O'Flanagan, riding his bicycle. I slowed my car down, to make sure it was indeed him. He was not my parish priest, but from a neighbouring parish, and a drinking partner of Father Mack.

A remote country lane, nobody about, a priest on a bicycle…all this too good to resist. Foot hard on the accelerator, I careered straight into Father Tom O'Flanagan, who was flung up in the air. I reversed, then ran over him, repeating this action, over and over. The mess on the tarmac was appalling. I managed to flatten his skull. His rib cage was also flattened. He could have been a cardboard cutout, except blood and entrails had spewed everywhere.

He was a total mess by the end I'd finished with him, totally unrecognizable from the tall fit looking priest that rode his bike, whenever he could. My car also got splattered with blood. A sudden almost biblical-like burst of rain washed his blood away, much to my relief.

The shockwave that hit the local area when his emaciated body was discovered was of epic proportions. It was obvious this was no hit and run accident,

The road was shut off, forensic police sent to do their job, then compressed bits and pieces of Father Tom O'Flanagan were gathered, the stain of his blood washed away, while the impact of his murder remained. My wife, as with previous incidents, was one of those who was in utter shock "Father Tom… who would wish to murder such a man" she said, tears forming in her eyes, thoroughly shaken. I half wanted to tell her, *darling it was me…*but I didn't, I wasn't through with my escapade. She never would have believed me anyway.

CHAPTER 4

A Heavy-Duty Confession.

Father Tom's replacement was a Father Patrick O'Shaughnessy. Considerably older than Father Tom, running Father O'Shaughnessy over on a bicycle seemed a closed opportunity, due to his bulky *physique.* Father O'Shaughnessy was so *overweight he* would be hard pressed to mount and ride a bicycle. I saw him a few times walking about the next town, offering an awkward smile as past people by. He quickly gained a reputation for being a *lacklustre* replacement for Father Tom, a priest who had been sent around many parishes, without ever leaving his mark.

The idea of "taking out" Father Tom's replacement had a great appeal, after all who would willingly want to take on the job of parish priest, after the predecessors had met horrific deaths? The job of being priest in this parish would be untenable, anyone who accepted the role would live in fear and would have to count on God to protect them.

I decided when the timing was right, I would pay Father Patrick, a visit…to make my confession. With my wife away visiting her elderly mother, an opportunity presented itself. I decided to go to Father Patrick's church, this time equipped with carefully selected "devices". I intended to use it during my *latest venture* into murder.

I arrived at such a time that I could ensure I was going to be the last in the confession box. When I was sure there was nobody about, I walked calmly to the confession box. I knelt and made the sign of the cross, almost ritualistically, as I had done many times before. My confession went like this…

"Forgive me, Father, for I have sinned. My last confession was five years ago, and these are my sins. My first major sin, committed last year was to inadvertently send a young prelate to his death, leaving him to suffer and excruciating death, while never informing the authorities. Then, a few months back there were the two gruesome murders of two priests in a church, both bludgeoned to death, I guess you read about this in the newspaper or saw it on television."

Father Patrick did not interrupt me, but I noted his breathing got progressively urgent. In the darkness of the confession box, I couldn't register his facial reaction to my very open confession.

"That's not all I said cheerfully, a few weeks ago there was Father Tom, I crushed him to pulp by running over him many times, I simply couldn't resist it."

"Now look here" interjected Father Patrick, snorting, his patience having run out. I was making mockery of some of the most heinous crimes in recent times. He bawled "The confession box in the house of God is no place for some kind sick joke!"

"This is no joke Father, you had better believe it." I said in a monotone voice.

Father Patrick was unnerved, he began to talk in an agitated voice, one evidently laced with a notable amount of anger.

"This is ridiculous, a grown man like you telling me sick infantile like lies… you should be ashamed of yourself, I suggest you leave, you disgust me".

"I do, do I?" I said… "but I am not leaving nor are you Father, you're staring death in the face, say your prayers Father, say your prayers."

"You're a lunatic man" blasted Father Patrick.

He kicked open the confessional door and imagined he could just walk away. He marched down the aisle, not realizing the two of us were alone and that he was at my mercy. I followed him calmly and as he reached to open the church door; I placed a cloth that had been dunked in chloroform over his pudgy face.

While the priest was out cold, I went to work. I tied him down to one of the pews. He was bulky and heavy to move, but I just about managed. Once secure I went to rummage about in the vestry. I yanked open a door to a cupboard and discovered it was not only full of alter wine, but the priest kept a fair stash of other alcohol, including whiskey. The man was quite obviously a closet alcoholic, I imagined a melancholic drunk. Under copies of The Irish Catholic Times, were some of the most hardcore pornography magazines I've ever seen. What kind of dirty man was this Father Patrick, I dreaded to think.

When Father Patrick was barely conscious, from my bag, I took put a hose pipe, about a meter long and a funnel which I attached to the hose pipe. Through his bleary eyes he must have seen me smiling. I coolly opened a bottle of alter wine, as if I was the host of a dinner party.

"Open wide Father" I said in the voice of a dentist. Father Patrick mumbled some inaudible words and then very obediently opened his mouth, perhaps still not realizing the precariousness of his situation. Having placed the pipe in his mouth I proceeded to pour half a bottle of wine down the funnel.

"Nice wine Father I said mockingly, adding, not vintage wine though, if truth be told."

Father Patrick was too busy coughing and spluttering

and trying to regain his breath.

"Want some more Father?" I said in the manner of a polite dinner party host. Father Patrick continued spluttering and didn't answer.

CHAPTER 5

Down the hatch.

With an unexpected surge of energy Father Patrick tried to break free, but I had done a first-rate job in efficiently securing him, having dragged him into the vestry and locked the doors.

"Stop this madness, right now" Father Patrick protested.

"I have only just started Father and judging by your secret stash, it seems you like a good tipple." I spoke sweetly as I prepared for round two, more from the same bottle.

"Down the hatch" I said having forced the end of the hose pipe into his mouth once again. Wine spewed out of his mouth; he couldn't take such a quantity in one go. His recovery time from this second "helping" was longer.

"Must be cheap wine Father, you don't seem to be enjoying our little drink together."

"Stop man for the love of God!" said the priest in a terrible state. "But Father, I sniggered, I seem to have uncovered your whisky, it's nice to have a little jolly on a Saturday afternoon, don't you think?"

I opened a fresh bottle of Irish whisky, quite a good quality as it happened, perhaps a gift from one his friends or a relation or perhaps in his desperation and loneliness he'd procured it himself.

I tipped the bottle casually down the funnel into the sozzled priest's mouth.

"Not such a bad way to meet your maker, eh Father, I mocked, the totally pissed priest. Father Patrick didn't respond. He started to violently spew up.

I shook my head.

"Oh, dear Father, you seem to be making a bit of a mess of yourself, can't hold your drink?"

After I had finished my caustic remark, another onslaught of vomit came out of Father Patrick's mouth. The smell was horrendous, but it didn't bother me. I persisted, with my crude torture.

"I guess you might fancy another drink having thrown up, eh Father?"

"No, no, for the love of God no". Father Patrick managed to say in a slurred voice that was hard to decipher.

"Don't be a kill joy Father, how about a bit more of this whisky, I imagine it's your favourite tipple."

I tipped the bottle once more and watched the agony of his face. I smelt the pungent smell of urine. He had wet himself.

"You dirty dog, you untrained puppy, you have wet yourself" I said in a scolding voice. I gave him no time to reply, I forced a bottle of neat gin down him. He was finished…but I wasn't finished. I began crumpling the porno mag pages up. When I had quite a stock, I forced the first one into his mouth. Then another and another.

He was soused. Death was staring him in the face. I grew tired of the force feeding and just whacked him with a chalice I had found attached to the vestry door. Blood spurted everywhere to join the river of vomit and alcohol. I put a large lit candle in his mouth, then I covered him with copies of "Swank" "Screw magazine" "Oui" and "Asian Babes". Now I was done, you can't inflict more pain on a dead man, I surmised.

I walked back to my car, looking out in case there were any onlookers, heading for the car, which I had hidden behind some trees. Father Patrick wasn't such a bad man, from what little I had experienced of him. I felt unexpected pangs of guilt. I had been excessive in the manner I had dispatched him, excessive being an understatement nevertheless killing priests had become all too routine.

CHAPTER 6

Unexpected changes.

Life appeared to be back to its monotonous routine, catching the same train, all those faces hidden behind newspapers, getting to work, then a tedious day of number crunching at Hawkings and Sproggat, getting the same train home, seeing Janet's dull friends on Saturdays, then church on Sunday. This was until I became aware of changes to my normal self. Firstly, I had these strong cravings for alcohol. This was hard to fathom, as I had never been a great drinker, the odd drop or two at a party, but never anything excessive. At first, I would down, a few glasses or two, when my wife was not about. However soon the situation seemed to dramatically worsen and added to this, despite my strong cravings I started to reject the alcohol, constantly rushing to the toilet to vomit. It was uncontrollable.

I even began this routine at work. I was sure my work colleagues would soon pick up on this. One remarked about the "stench" in the toilet. I was sure my wife would soon notice something was amiss. I tried to hide it from her as best I could, but it was getting an increasingly difficult task.

What was more I felt sure my appearance was changing. Flecks of grey hair suddenly appeared; despite the fact I'd always had a very youthful appearance. My face began to look more and more bloated. Was I dramatically aging?

My appearance was one thing, but there was more. One evening driving from work, I suddenly felt an urge to pull up at a newsagent. I would often buy my wife's gardening magazine or perhaps a golf magazine for me. I was suddenly drawn to the magazines on the top shelf and found myself shamelessly buying the latest editions of "Asian babes" "Asian fever" "Fetish weekly" and "Whiplash Monthly" some of Father Patrick's favourites.

In normal circumstances I would have found the images on the covers simply abhorrent and detestable. Quite simply I would never have been enticed to buy any magazine of this type. I still found my wife attractive, and we had an adequate sex life. However, here I was buying the most depraved magazines I could find, the shop supplied. I held a wad of magazines in my hand unabashed.

CHAPTER 7

A big let off.

Mr Ryan the newsagent fought hard to contain his surprise at my purchases. I could tell by the look he gave me when he handed me my change. I could guarantee without doubt, he had judged me as being a closet pervert. Mind you it was his shop that was the suppliers, so that said something about him. I flicked through the magazines in the car, half shocked, half enthralled. Later I made a quick visit to the off license, to acquire a small bottle of gin to meet my craving. I took a swig only to spew it all out, all over my suit. I set off. Maybe it was my erratic driving, I could not be sure, but I soon found myself tailed by a police car. I was signalled to stop.

Mr Respectable from leafy suburbia was now being stopped by the police. They hadn't found out about my priest killing fad…had they? This dark thought lurked in my mind, as I saw them move toward me. If they were to question me about my rampage of priest killings, how would I manage this situation? I was clueless.

"Step out the car, will you sir," said the taller of the two policemen. I did as I was told. I mumbled a pathetic excuse.

"I have been a bit sick officer, some terrible stomach bug I must have caught." The half empty bottle of whisky said otherwise. The police officers gave me a knowing look.

"We are going to have to breathalyse you sir, we have suspicions you have been drinking, we require you to do a test."

"Are you sure that is necessary" I said in my most

meek respectable middle-class voice.

"Yes sir, if you would kindly blow into this apparatus." The officer held out the apparatus; his face had a strong intent. I did as instructed.

The two police officers were surprised at the negative results.

"We'd like to take a look in your car sir." The taller one said, maybe not prepared for the stench that was about to greet him. They rummaged around, expecting to find drugs or some such, only to find some hardcore porn.

"You like this kind of thing do you sir…demanded the policeman waving a copy of Whiplash monthly, with a masked man wearing a rubber throng covering his genitals, lashing at a blond who had some torturous looking device attached to her nipples, while another masked man, legs apart appeared to enjoying fellatio, with the blond.

"Um, well not usually" I replied, feeling even more awkward.

"Live locally do you sir?" probed the policeman.

"Yes, I do" I replied sheepishly. The policeman glared at me "This is a respectable neighbourhood, sir, isn't it?" The policemen, said with menace in his voice.

"Yes, I believe so." I responded in a soft barely audible voice, my head bent down.

"Let's keep it that way, shall we?" said the taller policeman glaring at me. The policeman's radio began blaring away, apparently there were other urgent matters to deal with.

The two policemen, both obviously bemused walked solemnly back to their car and drove off much to my relief. For some reason my social credentials had saved me, or they could have caused me untold embarrassment. Perhaps they half admired my choice of pornography. I dumped the porn in the bin, but a few days later I felt an urge to buy more of the stuff. Soon I was surfing the internet to see if I could find even more salacious stuff than the type of the newsagent sold.

CHAPTER 8

Erratic behaviour.

My wife was getting increasingly concerned by my behaviour. On top of this I decided to make a momentous decision and quit my job. It came as a relief for my boss Mr Belmont. He helped me on my way, having called me into his office.

"You have becoming more and more erratic; rumours have been circulating you have been drinking at work. At first, I dismissed these kinds of rumours out of hand, you have always been one of the most reliable hard-working men we have had at this company. But recently I've had to question your behaviour. Looking for a document in a file in your office I hit upon "Miss Bondage Monthly" the most obscene magazine I have ever set my eyes on...I had the good fortune to meet Janet your charming wife, and she was a woman of the utmost propriety. I can't imagine why you would wish to look at such filth."

Belmont's face grew sterner, his anger intensified, "and then I found some stashed gin bottles." He shook his head. As you well know, totally against company policy."

Rather than listen to the rest of Belmont's "lecture" I left his office grabbed a few possessions (including Miss Bondage monthly) and was on my way, never to go back.

Telling my wife proved not so easy...

"How was your day, darling?" She inquired in the mechanical way, which I was accustomed to.

"Not so bad, darling, I have left my job" I replied in

an indifferent voice, as if relaying some unimportant news.

"You have quit Hawkings and Sproggat" she said in utter shock, looking like someone in the throes of a heart attack.

"You have worked there for thirteen years; in that time, you have had four promotions. I heard from Laura Hawkings when we were at the company gala you are held in great esteem, about to be fast tracked to the very top."

"It's just a job for Christ sakes Janet" I said sighing and shrugging my shoulders. Her mind was obviously working vigorously with all the connotations that would result from my new status of being unemployed.

"And what are we going to live on...I suppose you expect me to get a job!" The thought of her having to get a job troubled her greatly. My reply didn't really do much to alleviate her apprehensions. I said in a frivolous voice, with a caustic smile evident on my face.

"I am sure you could give up the Bridge club, sell your horse, meet your friends less, read less magazines on gardening, give up your life of leisure, instead of me providing for you."

My words stung her. After digesting what I had told her, she flew into a rage. It did not matter, however. I simply knew that with my new condition, I simply was incapable of doing any kind of job, let alone one that resembled my work at Hawkings and Sproggat, working on huge transactions.

Over days and weeks Janet's anger towards this sudden change in my behaviour led us to be increasingly more distant. We had become strangers. I wasn't concerned with the future; I was more interested in navigating in the present. A few arguments later, my wife soon left me, saying she was going to "live with her mother" until I was able to "get my life together and start to resemble the man she'd married".

The house felt very empty, without Janet, not that I resented her absence. No job, no wife, my life mostly consisted of reading hardcore (the more hardcore the better) pornography. This was accompanied by a new obsession…going to church. I would go at every opportunity…but why? I asked myself this question over and over again. It wasn't guilt for those priests I had killed…though this was etched in my past…I was done with priests, or so I thought…no there was another dark deeper guilt I carried, to do with Father Patrick's past life, but for the moment I was unable to bring to light.

CHAPTER 9

A disturbing dream.

It was a vivid dream that revealed the essence of this guilt. It all began quite happily. I was an adolescent, with a group of friends fishing. We were smoking rolled up cigarettes, while laughing and joking. We were by the sea. This joyful mood was soon interrupted by screams and panic coming from a group of holiday makers. I rushed with my band of male friends to the site of what was obviously a tragedy. A beautiful young girl, maybe ten years old, in the dream, had been discovered drowned, her body limp and lifeless. On further inspection of the girl, I came to a stark conclusion. It was my younger sister who had perished.

My torment was overwhelming, for it was I who was supposed to be caring for her. I had left her on the beach, saying I was just going to say hello to a few friends, not realizing she would go swimming in a hazardous area which had accounted for the lives of many a reckless swimmer. I knew I had the daunting task of facing my mother.

On hearing the news my mother was inconsolable. Her pain was soon followed by acrimony.

"Paddy you were supposed to be looking after the girl, I told both you and her, never to swim, at high tide in the cold."

"I'm so sorry Mammy, I wept…just so sorry."

My apologies were not good enough. She slapped me in the face, not once but many times. Her beloved daughter dead, all because I went off to see my friends and neglected a simple responsibility.

Then the dream moved onto the funeral of my sister…Caitlin was her name. Little Caitlin swept out to sea, spotted by some fisherman, while her brother drank and smoked and jerked about with adolescent friends…

After the funeral had finished my mother looked me straight in the eye and said "Patrick, you might be able to make your peace with God, but you will never make your peace with me!"

I woke up with a start. Who was I? Michael Dawkins, a respectable (well at least in former times) suburban dweller. Or Patrick O'Shaughnessy, a dead priest who seemed to be taking over my mind body and soul and now my dreams.

CHAPTER 10

To Quell My Curiosity.

I decided to make a trip to Ireland. Father Mack, now a rather old and decrepit priest had unwittingly told me the name of Father Patrick's birthplace, a small fishing town called Kilmore quay in the south of Ireland. Father Mack had grown up in the same village, an apparent breeding ground for priests…

When I arrived, I asked around, about the O'Shaughnessy family, the son had been a priest, unfortunately a murdered priest. People thought I was an investigator, I certainly felt unwanted. After a couple of days, I went to a library. The woman in the library proved more forthcoming, directing me to a section with the local newspapers. Looking through the archives of local newspapers, I discovered Clodagh O'Shaunessy, Father Patrick's mother was long dead, but she had a niece living in Killmore Quay.

I had to work out some kind of strategy. Journalist no…an author writing about the locals of Killmore Quay? A historian sounded plausible. It didn't matter anyway. Nora O'Shaughnessy was totally mad, but at least I managed to track her down. She welcomed me heartily. I could have been The Pope; it was that kind of cheerful welcome.

The conversation veered off in different tangents before I slipped the name Clodagh into the conversation. Nora shook her head several times, her eyes lighting up. "A bad penny our Aunt Clodagh, who could have imagined having two children by a priest no less. Unthinkable in those days. My mother would hardly mention her name. Then again, she suffered, more than most women would suffer. Her daughter swept away at sea, Caitlin was her name, the poor little lamb should have been looked after, went for a swim at Devil's Dyke, discovered by holidaymakers so they say. A sad story."

"There was a brother" I interjected.

"Yes…Patrick, the scallywag was supposed to care for young Caitlin, but was with his friends, drinking so they say, never managed to live with his shame, a few years later crossed the sea and became a priest, met a terrible ending so I heard…this family is full of woe.

I listened to her ranting for a while, before making my excuses and leaving, equipped with all the information I had come for. My visit had made me aware of the fact that Father Patrick had become a priest on two counts, to make up for his father had been a defiled priest and his residing guilt over his little sister. It seemed now as if I was to carry this guilt.

CHAPTER 11

Being Patrick O'Shaunessy.

Who could I turn to? I could hardly tell a living soul I was slowly slipping into being a priest I had killed. I had to accept that now I was Patrick O'Shaunessy...In consequence my life now involved, going to church twice a day...to ask forgiveness for a sin I had never committed. This along with drinking. Consequently, throwing up lots of alcohol and gawping at copious amounts of hardcore porn...All of this until my savings run dry. There was also the strong possibility Janet, might justifiably squeeze me dry in the divorce courts, we'd been apart for quite a while....

Regardless of my fears I started to dress how I imagined Patrick O'Shaunessy might dress, wearing sombre black of grey colours. I began to engage in long conversations, sometimes out loud, sometimes in my head, with Caitlin...

Caitlin, I was such an eejit, playing the big man, with me friends, when I should have been looking after you, my dear sister, for the love of God, can you forgive me, Paddy's an eejit, pure and simple, always playing the joker, trying to impress his friends, you do understand this, sweet girl...

All the time I was putting on more and more weight, my face bloating and yet I hardly ate all day. It wouldn't be long before I would replicate Father Patrick's size. Even my accent started to have a slight Irish lilt about it. I had to contain this, when Janet called, it was a hard-fought battle. I hoped that she had not picked up on this new development.

Once Janet arrived unexpectedly, she'd come to pick

up some things and to pick up Merlin, our dog (she doubtlessly couldn't trust me with a dog…she had good reasons). She found me sat in the living room, dressed in black, with an Irish folk tune blaring, flicking through "Tight love Bondage" magazine, my trousers around my ankles.

She stared at me, in total disbelief, her revulsion was totally understandable and justified. "Michael, you disgust me" she screamed in a voice that must have easily reached neighbours' ears, before bursting out of the house as quickly as she'd arrived, dragging Merlin, less he got perverted.

I just sat looking up at the ceiling concluding my life was on a downward slope and there were ropes to hold myself from sinking further. In fact, I had been saner I was slaughtering priests.

CHAPTER 12

A Time to Confess

One morning on a whim I thought I might go to confession, at Father Mack's church. I'd always rather liked Father Mack, despite his long-winded sermons. There would be no instruments of death or forced alcohol. I thought it might be fun to admit to some of those heinous sins, to gauge his reaction.

But then again, I might try and get some new snippets on Father Patrick, another of my obsessions.

I wanted to know more about the man...I couldn't get enough of this man; I was so tied to him. Perhaps of all the priests I slayed, this one had seemed the most prosaic, just an ordinary parish priest, who'd been sent here and there without ever excelling and yet I had (by killing him) discovered this complex interesting character, a porno loving priest, who had other even darker secrets and guilt, the death of his sister, and was this on top of being stigmatized, the bastard son of a Catholic priest.

I drew up at the church, as usual there weren't too many takers for confession. I said a few prayers, again asking to be pardoned for my neglect of Christ's very own angel Caitlin. It was soon my turn.

I began...

"Forgive me, Father, for I have sinned. My last confession was a day ago and these are my sins." I had unavoidably slipped into an Irish accent. I could hear Father Mack's wheezy breath. The confessional was as dark as ever.

Suddenly Father Mack spoke, cutting me off before I

could speak. "Patrick…Patrick, I know why you are here, but the Lord will never forgive you…you and I were both there that day, we both know what went on, what you did is worse than unforgivable."

I responded as Patrick O'Shaunessy surely would have. In recent weeks my mind had re-enacted that day by the beach, with young Patrick and his friends.

I began protesting in a quiet desperate voice.

"But Father, I just left Caitlin for a time, we were young lads, having a laugh, having a few beers…"

"That's what you told your Mammy Patrick, but we know different, now don't we?" Father Mack said in an accusative voice. *Oh no,* I thought, it's worse than I imagined, Father Patrick had done something even more wicked…

"You were always jealous of young, sweet Caitlin. Your Mammy loved her so much more than you, even as a youngster you must have known this."

Father Mack drew in a deep breath before he continued. "So, what do you do… you trick sweet, innocent Caitlin into swimming further than she should have, knowing full well she feared the sea and wasn't a good swimmer. I saw the tears in her eyes as she set off, but you were laughing at her with the others, as you still were, watching her struggle with the waves.

Then you even went as far as taking bets with your friends, as to whether she would make it back alive. When you realised what you had done, when you saw the coastguards dragging her listless body back to shore, it was too late.

Who was worse me the priest killer or Father Patrick, who'd sent his younger sister off to a certain death out of sheer jealousy. Of course, numerically my crimes were far greater, but to kill your own flesh and blood…

"You good as murdered that young girl, she was beginning to get far more attention than you, everybody loved her, she was due a happy life, but you took that away from her, and when they buried your sister, they may as well have buried your Mammy, such was her grief."

CHAPTER 13

Drowning in my Own Guilt.

I found myself sobbing, and as I did, I started to become aware of water racing down the walls of the confessional box. It was sea water, it just kept oozing out of the confession box walls. Quickly it was up to my knees. I just imagined that I could open the door and get out of the confession box...but no it was jammed. I tried to kick at the door, using all my force as the water kept rising, there was no exit. Next, I shrieked at Father Mack as the water mounted.

"Father, for God's sake let me out."

Father Mack stayed as calm as ever, as if he was still listening to my (or rather Father Patrick's confession). I began to become desperate.

"I'm not Patrick Father, my name is Michael, you have got me confused with a priest you knew..." My words did little good, the icy water kept rising, it would soon be up to my shoulders. Drowning in a confessional box, I could never have anticipated that...but this seemed to be my reality. Father dismissed the pleas concerning my true identity.

"Don't be silly Patrick" he snapped.

"I'm going to drown Father...this confessional box seems to be filling up with sea water if you don't do something." I glanced through the curtain in the confessional at Father Mack had not one drop on him, (the water did not seem to permeate through to him, for some inexplicable reason) still sat calmly.

"What shall we do take bets on how long it will take" sneered Father Mack. "Have a few beers, smoke a few roll ups." I was in no mood for sarcastic barbs.

"Father, for pity's sake help me." I yelled, as water swelled beyond my chin. In seconds I would be fighting for breath. I heard Father Mack muttering something about the water finally washing away the sins of my past. I was soon spluttering, having to try to arch myself upwards to catch my breath. Within moments I was totally submerged by the water and in total darkness.

I struggled and struggled until my life began slipping away.

I blacked out.

CHAPTER 14

Where the hell am I?

When I came round, I found myself in a white room. My first inclination was that I was in a secure psychiatric hospital. The insane priest killer locked up for good, banished from society, shortly to be damned to Hell. But no…There was no bars on the windows, I wasn't secured to my bed. Though I was obviously pumped up with drugs and very groggy, there was the strong whiff of a hospital, as well as hospital looking gadgetry.

I was left in my own thoughts for a time, still coming to terms with my new situation when I heard voices, one of which was very familiar, that of my wife Janet. Had she arrived equipped with a divorce lawyer? No, she stood alongside a young doctor at the foot of my bed for a moment just looking at me, with pity in her eyes.

"Oh Michael" she said with a voice filled with emotion. She gripped my hand. A tear of joy slipped down her face.

"You were a lucky man" said the young doctor with a beaming smile.

"You must be still a bit dazed and confused…you went for a walk with your dog in appalling weather, there was a massive storm, you must have tripped up on some wire, your head hit a rock, luckily you were discovered by a passerby, who alerted the emergency services and finally you were brought here, to this hospital. You have a nasty gash on your head, but it should heal, but we need to do some scans."

This revelation took time to sink in, but in a way, it was a relief.

"So, I am not the priest killer" I said in a hushed voice.

Janet went quiet for a moment.

"What in God's name are you talking about?" My wife said with a shrill voice, at my unprompted bizarre proclamation. The doctor sighed and said, "don't worry Mrs Dawkins, you have to expect him to not his normal self, it's quite common in these kinds of cases, he's been through quite a trauma." Janet wasn't convinced and still looked very disturbed.

CHAPTER 15

A strange kind of familiarity.

So began some numbingly boring days in hospital. On a drab Monday morning, while I struggled to read a dull murder mystery, which Janet had brought me. There was a knock on the door and in walked a young man I recognized immediately even though I had never set eyes on him before, well not in the real world, at least.

"I'm the man who discovered you Mr. Dawkins, I've just came to see how you are." The young man said with a nervous look on his face.

"You're from Poland, aren't you?" I blurted out.

"Yes, he replied, how do you know…my accent perhaps?" "I know a lot about you…I said with a slight smile, you are training to be a priest."

The young man looked at me in bemusement, as if I was somehow about to unravel his whole life, although in his mind I was a complete stranger.

"You are the oldest son, you moved to England five years ago with your family, you wanted to go out with an English girl, but your parents wouldn't allow you, and now you are a priest's seminary, but you have grave doubts about being a priest…am I right?"

The young man looked at me stunned. A long silence ensued followed by a stifled conversation. I thanked him for saving me; he told me God had smiled on me that day. If he hadn't heard my dog barking, he would never have discovered me, certainly not in a storm like that.

As he was about to leave, I impertinently said, "you don't really want to be a priest, now, do you?" He didn't answer, he just closed the door behind him and went on his way. A few days later I was told I was going to be moved to another room and would share it with another patient. The hospital was short of beds. The other patient I was told about had suffered a severe head injury, as well as other serious l injuries. His condition was such that he would be unable to communicate with me, certainly not at this moment in time. From what I gathered I was about to share my room with a living vegetable.

Though I had never met him in the flesh, I was about to re-encounter Father Tom. It felt strange having this presence in my room that only made wheezing noises, incapable of communicating. This kind of suited me. What had happened to him? I asked the doctor. "Some drunken maniac knocked him off his bicycle, ran him over a number of times, for some unknown reason, left him for dead."

"Oh" I said, feeling somewhat familiar with what had been described to me, however he seemed to have come off a little better than the flattened version I had last envisaged. He still looked an awful sight and a pathetic looking entity.

One afternoon, I was disturbed by a knock on the door; Father Mack charged in the room. He was paying a visit to Father Tom. Rather futile I thought because Father Tom was still in this comatose state.

Father Mack tried talking to him normally... "How you are faring Father Tom...we miss you; your parishioners all miss you, Mrs Hockings sends her best wishes, you need to get well soon, back on your feet, eh Father."

It was all useless, there were no signs of recognition, but Father Mack persisted, almost out of obligation.

When he realized he might as well be talking to the wall, he turned to me.

"You had a terrible accident Mr Dawkins, I heard, you were discovered by a young Pole, training to be a priest."

"That's right Father, I had a lucky escape."

"God must have looked down on you" said the priest cheerfully. Father Tom, appears not so lucky, mown down by some maniac, he'll be here a long time."

His voice hushed. "Perhaps will never be his normal self, poor man."

"So, I have heard Father" I replied, sighing, as if to show mutual concern."

"In fact, a replacement is being shipped over from Ireland, an old acquaintance of mine a Father Patrick O'Shaunessy, known him since childhood."

"Oh, really Father" I said, adding "that will be nice for you."

After a moment I piped up, saying I wonder if it's the same Patrick O'Shaunessy my friends from Killmore Quay told me about, the one whose sister died tragically? Quite the local figure, from what I understand. Father didn't reply. His focus was on Father Tom, who had begun to make gurgling sounds. He sighed, shrugged his shoulders in despair, said a quick goodbye and then wandered off.

CHAPTER 16

Making Father Jethro Squirm.

A doctor informed me that I was going to be kept over Christmas, a precaution I was told, was necessary with my kind of head injury and delirium. A few days before Christmas, I (and Father Tom) had a visitor, a Father Jethro, arrived. With a broad smile he told me he was visiting a few patients in the ward, but the main purpose of his visit was a grand carol service that a young choir was going to perform. He'd been told I could be wheeled out, to the concert hall to enjoy a bit of Christmas celebrations. Father Jethro, was good-looking young and very smug, began to annoy me. I'd been happy on my own (Father the vegetable Tom wasn't any sort of company). I had not expected any visitors; Janet had said she was busy all day.

Suddenly I blurted out, in the voice of a teenager... "Father, will you be my Facebook friend?"

Father Jethro recoiled, looked at me shocked, his previous panache severely blunted. He laughed awkwardly.

"Why of course, if you wish..." I wanted to reinforce his discomfort, in a most cutting manner.

"Oh Father, I thought you only really liked young girls, they certainly seem to like you, eh Father..."

"I am not sure I know what you are talking about" said the priest irked. I shook my head and tutted before saying.

"I think you do Father; I think you enjoy the attention you get, a handsome priest like you..."

Father Jethro didn't stay long. He charged out of the room, without saying another word. I went to the concert, of course my focus was on Father Jethro, who unsurprisingly seemed to be rather sour faced throughout, his mind was preoccupied. I happily concluded; I had touched a nerve. The carols were dreary, the performance insipid. At the end, Father Jethro averted my gaze and made a hasty exit, no doubt glad to get out of my presence.

CHAPTER 17

Back Home.

After a most dreary Christmas, as the new year approached, I was deemed well enough to go home. It felt strange being back at home with Janet. It was like I was being appended to a stranger, even though we had been together for many years. My time in hospital had felt like a great chasm and had created a distance between us, as if I had to get to know her again. Of course, she was a reliable steady woman, but at the same time she was rather uninspiring. I was back to middle class mediocrity. I tried to be enthusiastic during any conversation with Janet, but it sometimes proved laborious.

After an appropriate period of recuperation, I was back at my job at Hawkings and Sproggat and my mind-numbing existence, away from the turbulent but exhilarating exploits of the priest killer and no longer uncovering Father Patrick's duplicitous life. I certainly would not be putting porn in the filing cabinet or drinking and throwing up in the toilets…though all of this seemed quite tempting.

Though I just about managed to knuckle down to my job, there were these deep lurking feelings of antipathy towards priests that seemed to manifest every time I had any kind of contact. Father Tom had one foot in the grave anyway, why not help him along the way?

Father Jethro, that irksome choir master I had ascertained, was more into winning the favour of love-struck teenagers, he really irked me. I had a good mind to track him down, and dish out what he deserved, he'd suffer I'd make sure of it, this time it would be for real! I could save that young Polish prelate from being trapped in a life he hadn't chosen, a life that would probably only bring him misery. Then there's Father Mack, I was still being dragged along by my wife to Sunday services. I couldn't face looking at the confessional, not after my drowning experience which still haunts me.

Perusing through my life, it is priests that agitate me the most. I am now being obligated by voices raging in my head, telling me to go out and set about what I must do, seeking fulfilment through wanton carnage. Yes, believe me I am the priest killer, my soul is dark and profane.

PART 2

CHAPTER 18

A Lady Priest Killer

Passion of a forbidden kind.
Italy 1892

My name is Lucrezia Di Benevento, and my soul is black and damned many times over. When I was sixteen years old my father told me I was so beautiful I could take my pick of any man in the land. But my heart was set on somebody who was totally forbidden, I chose a priest.

Most of my childhood was spent being brought up in the confines of a nunnery. My main contact with men was a tenuous one with priests. Often in my dreams I had visions of Angelo Amentini, a young seminarian.

All the girls had eyes for this young priest. In my dreams he often repeated the same refrain "release me". What did he mean by this? In reality my one exchange with him was the catechism classes he undertook on a Saturday morning. My mind was never centered on what he was saying, it was more on his voice, his looks and what it would be like to spend time alone with him.

The young seminarian seemed to lack confidence. Did he really want to be a priest? Perhaps he had been forced into it. When he arrived at the nunnery, he'd sent a ripple of gossip among the girls. I wasn't the only one he made an instant impression on. Albertina Mondellio had been overheard whispering wild suppositions about him by Sister Josepha during evening prayers. She had been sent to the Reverend Mother who had wrapped her hand six times with a ruler. Her hand was swollen, the pain lasting long after the punishment.

"Angelo Amentini is training to be a man of God and should not be the subject of lurid conversations between young girls who should be more attentive to learning the word of God" exclaimed the fiery Reverend Mother.

When Sister Clotilde's beady eyes caught sight of a note being passed from Allegra Santini to Santuzza Della Bona, without warning she marched straight to the Reverend Mother's office, with the note firmly gripped in her hand, shaking with fury.

"Your eyes like deepest sapphire.
My heart beats for you Angelo,
I imagine us walking hand in hand
under a moonlit sky.
My love for you knows no bounds.
Hold me tight, sweet Angelo,
Let me feel the vigour of your kiss,
Let our bodies join in rapture."

It was the last line that particularly enraged the Reverend Mother. She stormed out of her office and rushed to the classroom where she grabbed Allegra and Santuzza by the ears, before dragging them screaming to her office. Taking an eighteen inch stick she began thrashing first Allegra and then Santuzza. The girl's shrieks of pain resonated around the school.

Worse was to come, the Reverend Mother reached into her drawer and grabbed a pair of scissors. Grabbing Allegra by the hair, she began to hack at her beautiful locks of blond hair.

"No Reverend Mother!" pleaded Allegra to no avail.

The Reverend pointed the scissors first at Allegra's eyes and then at Santuzza's eyes.

"Take your punishment you wicked girls, or I will

have reason to gauge out your evil eyes" Sister Clotilde felt duty bound to try to intercede. She anticipated correctly the Reverend Mother was now out of control.

This was no ordinary punishment she was dishing out; this was hateful violence. Sister Clotilde worried for the girl's safety. She had often witnessed the Reverend Mother in one of her moods, but this seemed to go well past the limit of anything she'd seen before.

Her lame attempts to intercede on the girl's behalf failed miserably. The Reverend Mother carried on telling Sister Clotilde not to interfere. She continued hacking at Allegra's hair, while shouting at the two victims to hold their tongues.

Allegra wept hysterically, while Santuzza pleaded with the Reverend Mother to be spared the same treatment.

There was no abating in the Reverend Mother's vicious onslaught; Santuzza got exactly the same treatment. The two girls were then ordered to go to the shower rooms, where they were told to strip naked. The Reverend Mother turned on the cold shower and loose remnants of hair were washed away, while the two girls shrieked and shivered under the freezing water. The Reverend Mother then marched the two girls, holding onto their clothes and stood them in front of all of us, who just looked on in amazement. Both girls had great bald patches on their scalps, their remaining hair had been cropped to the limit. Both girls were still crying. It took them months to regain their composure, but the mental scars from that night lived with them forever. This still did not stop me from desiring Angelo.

Being able to see the young seminarian, was a more trying matter, under the threat of the Reverend Mother discovering some kind of liaison. The same fate that had befallen Allegra and Santuzza hung over me. Discretion and perseverance were the best approach. I would soon be finishing my schooling at the nunnery. I had to keep my feelings for Angelo in check. Most girls could barely look at the young seminarian, let alone engage in any conversion, other than one of a strictly religious bearing.

When I finally completed my studies at the nunnery I began a long period of social events, as my parents initiated the search for a suitable husband. My sisters were all married to suitable spouses and had begun the process of providing for heirs. I found each social event uninspiring. Even though I had a legion of men surrounding me, openly flirting with me, I soon tired of this. All these young men seemed to fall short of the mark and none of them ignited my interest. I batted them away. One by one, I killed any of their hopes of winning my heart.

CHAPTER 19

The Wedding.

One day father showed me a wedding invitation. The daughter of Duke Di Lucca was going to marry Giuseppe Di Benvento. The two who were about to marry were of little interest to me, despite father's enthusiasm for the significance of the union. It was the priest who was to marry them, that held my fascination, it was Father Angelo Amentini.

The time could not pass quickly enough till the day of the marriage.

I made great efforts to look my best, whilst in Venice I bought a dress made of silk taffeta, adorned with antique rose-point lace and pearls. I insisted that a famous coiffeur come all the way from Rome, to do my hair on the day of the wedding. My parents complained it wasn't my marriage!

My parents could not understand why I had placed so much importance on my attire and appearance for this wedding, when previously I had shown scant enthusiasm. On the day I sprayed ample amounts of perfume which had been ordered from Paris, a fine perfume that had elements of fern, citrus, lavender and geranium as well as amber, musk and oakmoss.

When I was finally ready to leave, my parents were amazed, my father said, partly in jest, that I would make the bride feel wholly inadequate. As we waited in the church for the ceremony to begin, I noticed many of the congregation's eyes latching on me. The men gawped in stark admiration, the women in obvious envy.

Father Angelo walked in, with magnificent robes, a

white cope embroidered with an intricate gold design. He looked fresh-faced as ever and extremely handsome. There seemed to be an element of fear that was spread across his face, while he primed himself for the ceremony he was about to perform. Those feelings I'd had for him while in the nunnery were reignited. I could not keep my eyes off him, while my imagination ran wild.

My father whispered in my ear. "Lucrezia you are staring at the young priest." I ignored father's remark, but I knew what he had said was the truth, I could not help myself. The bride walked in, on the arm of father while the groom waited, organ music droned on.

There seemed to be tension in the church, as Angelo waited to begin the ceremony. His voice was unsure, I got the impression he was shaking with nerves. I would have loved to have tried to calm his nerves or better still take him away from this ordeal. He stuttered uneasily during his address, there was a palpable unease throughout. At the end of the ceremony, I could see the relief at its conclusion, written on his face, his duties were done.

I saw him standing outside the church, he seemed isolated and awkward. He let out an occasional smile of recognition to some of the congregation. I felt a strong urge to talk to him, but I anticipated there would be other opportunities. I also took comfort in the fact that now I knew how to contact him.

I sneaked a glance at him as our family carriage sped off to the reception. It proved boring at first, endlessly shaking hands with various acquaintances, father and mother encouraging me to get acquainted to various men, including the groom's brother, naturally eligible, a huge local landowner and at present an officer serving in the army.

Suddenly my eyes caught sight of Angelo, standing alone on the periphery. I excused myself from my parents and the military man and crossed the grand hall and stood in front of Angelo. I didn't care about any reaction my behavior might stir from my parents and other onlookers. Angelo was taken aback by her sudden appearance.

"Do I know you?" he stuttered.

"Maybe you don't remember me, we met under rather different circumstances, I was a pupil at the Istituto Sacro Cuore, we never spoke as such, except in confines of the classroom."

Angelo nodded his head gently. I wondered if he still dwelt on his time at the school and the furore, he had caused not only among the girls but doubtlessly among some of the nuns.

I also pondered on the fact that inadvertently two girls had been punished severely on account of a letter, which had been written in his honour. Did he realize how much power he held over us girls? That we would have done anything for him? That while we were in his lessons or in church as he helped during mass, our minds were preoccupied with him and not on spiritual matters. His sheer presence had changed so much at the school it had created an underlying heavy atmosphere of sexual tension.

"I'm sorry I don't recall your face, there were many girls I had the pleasure of teaching the word of God to."

I found his reply disappointing, but was prepared to persist, even if it meant I had to break through his cold facade. I thought I might try some flattery, even though it was blatantly unjustifiable.

"I enjoyed the service, I said with a spurious smile,

Father, you conducted the ceremony in a most reverent and appropriate way." The young priest blushed, perhaps he was still thinking about the inept way he'd muddled his way through.

"That is most kind of you to say," he said earnestly, "I am a new servant of God, and this is the first time I have presided over the sacrament of marriage."

Our conversation proved highly inhibited, but I laboured on, none the less.

Angelo's life revolved around the church and his vocation as a priest, and it was hard to draw him away from this subject. He remained painfully uncomfortable in my presence. In one last attempt to loosen him up, I suggested I get him a glass of wine.

"I believe even Jesus provided and drank wine in a wedding, did he not?"

"It's true, but I am not a great wine drinker I am afraid. I always believe in moderation." Shaking his head, "I have seen many a man's souls darkened by the effects of alcohol."

"You drink alter wine, don't you?" I demanded. My frivolity niggled him.

"I drink the blood of Christ, that is different" he replied.

"I imagine you spend long evenings by yourself, I said with a vague smile, how do you pass such time?"

"I am often in deep reflection, or praying, the priest sighed, perhaps I read a book to increase my wisdom and spiritual awareness, I have no time to waste," he said earnestly.

"But you must get lonely, feel a need for company?" I tested him.

"I have very few requirements, he said solemnly, I have my housekeeper and occasional visits from parishioners, who require enlightenment or advice on spiritual matters."

"You have no regrets giving up your life for God?" I probed him even deeper and noticed his facial expression barely registered the remotest change, despite the brusqueness of my question. Probing further I said, "you will never have the warmth of a female's touch or have the possibility of having children to fill your life with joy."

The young priest shrugged, "I am amply compensated by my devotion to God and my rewards if I remain true to his name will be a life eternal" He sounded as if he was doggedly repeating the words from a book, he had read many times over.

Our conversation seemed to be hurtling down a cul-de-sac, when the military man, the groom's brother, and best man, joined us.

"How are you Angelo, or should I say Father Angelo" the young officer asked.

"I am fine Lucius and you?"

The military man smiled, "Feeling splendid especially standing next to such a beautiful young woman, don't you agree Angelo, or does your faith exclude you from admiring such beauty?"

"You never were one for subtlety Lucius" Angelo muttered, with a notable tinge of disdain. I looked at the two men noting striking similarities.

"You two know each other" I butted in, a second glance confirming what I had already remarked upon.

"We are cousins, are we not Angelo,"

He turned to face me.

"I don't believe I have the pleasure in knowing your name, young lady."

"My name is Lucrezia Del Petruso and my father as I

am sure you are aware is Count Del Petruso".

"A pretty name to suit such a beautiful face".

His arrogance was overbearing, but at least I would be able to have a conversation unlike the monosyllabic chat from Angelo.

"You flatter me, but shouldn't you show a bit more decorum as we are both standing close to a man of God," The officer sighed, "maybe you're right said the young officer, with a sardonic smile, maybe I should whisk you away to the dance hall, I hear the orchestra are now ready to start the proceedings, my name is Lucius Di Benvento."

"What if I choose not to dance with you" I said, with a half-smile, trying to dampen his natural exuberance.

"Then I shall leave you in the company of Cousin Angelo, he replied grinning, ruing the lost opportunity of a dance with a cavalry officer, who many women would have a bare fist fight in order to have the chance of a dance."

"Your arrogance knows no bounds," I complained.

"But it won't stop you from dancing with me, I hear the orchestra are now playing one of my favourite waltzes."

Defying any form of etiquette, he took hold of my hand and gently led me away from Angelo, towards the dance hall. A few eyes followed us as we weaved our way through a melange of people, into the impressive dance hall.

He was an assured dancer, in the same way, that he was a confident speaker. For a time, I put Angelo to the back of my mind and enjoyed the moment. We danced together over a considerable period of time. When we stopped, he went in search of some wine. He told me he was often away on long missions. His bravery was obvious, he had medals to show this, pinned onto his bright tunic.

Once he had returned holding two glasses of wine our conversation turned to Angelo. I explained that I had encountered Angelo before, that I had been taught by nuns and that he had spent some time at the school, while he was still a seminary.

"Lucky him, who wouldn't be happy spending their time in the company of young girls".

CHAPTER 20

The Disappearance.

"He's not easy to talk to," I said of Angelo, with a frown.

"He's always been a somewhat complex character, even as a young boy," said the officer, shaking his head. Let me tell you a story about Angelo when we were boys. Poor Angelo often suffered from ill health. He even spent time in various sanatoriums. Mother even told me on occasions he was close to death. When he was about fifteen, he came to stay with our family, because his parents were on a short trip abroad.

My brother Giuseppe and I had planned a camping trip, which would involve hunting some wolves, lynx and wild boar at night. We certainly hadn't envisaged Angelo coming with us. He would undoubtedly have been a burden. He insisted on joining us, despite our protests to our parents.

Why our parents agreed to him coming with us, I can't imagine. He was unused to outdoor life and then there was his ill health that could manifest itself. Maybe Angelo himself wanted to prove a point, that he wasn't just a sickly boy.

We set off early in the morning, it was going to be a long hike to the base camp where we would be staying a couple of days. We took some provisions, to make sure we would eat properly, if we couldn't find enough food in the forest. Angelo lagged behind us and hardly uttered a word. My brother and I called him "the choir boy" or "the little angel" much to his displeasure. He looked so sweet and innocent.

He was slightly younger than us, but we were far

worldlier. He seemed to have a dogged determination, to be equal to us, his cousins, we are being noted for our hardiness. It was a hot day and flies kept buzzing around us as we trudged deeper into the forest.

To amuse ourselves sometimes we would quicken the pace to create a distance between ourselves and Angelo, to try to see the panic it would create for Angelo. When he started to shout our names, we would jump from behind a bush and scream wildly "little angel", causing a combination of fear and apoplexy. We arrived wearily at our destination and went about setting up our camp. Around a campfire, we mercilessly made fun of Angelo.

'Do you like girls Angelo?'

'Ever touched a girl?'

'Do you prefer boys?'

Each question made Angelo squirm. Did he regret joining us I wondered. We decided to go for a swim in the pond. Needless to say, we pushed Angelo in fully clothed, he emerged out of the water covered in algae and duckweed. Again, he cursed us.

"He is your cousin," I interrupted, pulling a face.

"It is true, but we were boys who loved high jinks and we were not so fond of this cousin, who seemed far too sensitive and sedate for our taste. After the swim, while warming up by the campfire, my brother decided to open a glass of wine he had procured from my parent's sizeable cellar."

'Some wine Angelo' he said buoyantly. Angelo seemed unsure of himself.

'I have never had wine, apart from wine during mass.'

'Well, it's about time you did' replied Giuseppe as he poured three sizeable glasses of wine. Giuseppe and I sunk our glasses quickly, Angelo was more cautious, but in time he'd consumed two glasses.

We went to sleep late into the night and woke up long after the sun had risen. We ate some rolls and fruit we had brought with us. Angelo seemed to be suffering. The wine had taken its toll, indeed he seemed to be struggling the whole day long. He spent most of the day reading a book, while Giuseppe and I tried to catch some fish from the languid pond. As light began to diminish, we prepared for our night of hunting.

Giuseppe knew the forest well and we marched quietly behind him. After a moment we became aware of sporadic drops of rain. Suddenly there was a great downpour and constant thunder. We hadn't anticipated a sudden storm of biblical proportions. The torrential rain was relentless.

Giuseppe and I raced towards the wooden shack where we were camping; we didn't realize that Angelo could not keep up with us. When we became aware of his absence it was too late. The storm was causing devastating damage, paths were being washed away, the conditions were appalling, with storm damage everywhere.

We decided after a while to try to search for him, despite all the possible dangers and destruction. We screamed his name as we cautiously made our way through the forest. All was to no avail. We made our way back to the shack waiting for the storm to abate. In the morning, we made a fresh search, which again proved fruitless. We decided we should make our way back home to call for help.

When we broke the news that Angelo was missing our parents were first shocked and then scolded us for not looking after him. Within a short time, a sizeable search party was assembled. A message was sent to inform Angelo's parents of his absence. Giuseppe and I were devastated and anxious for any news of Angelo's well-being.

The first day of the search had proved worthless, by the third day all hope was but lost. Even with sniffer dogs and foresters and military personnel, nobody could find a trace of Angelo, he seemed to have all but disappeared. The search was given up. Giuseppe and I could hardly deal with weight of having not looked after our younger cousin, the guilt was unbearable, I heard Giuseppe crying at night, totally out of character, as the Giuseppe I was more familiar with was always a robust unshakable individual.

We were having dinner, all of us were solemn, hardly a word was spoken, everybody's mind was on the absent Angelo, fearing he must have perished. Suddenly we were aware of some agitation, one of the servants, called Rossi, burst into the dining room.

'He's alive, he's back' he shouted in disbelief.

'Thanks be to God!' exclaimed mother and father almost in tandem.

We all watched in amazement as Angelo walked hesitantly into the room. He looked dishevelled and had a slight cut on his face. Mother stood up and went towards him putting her arms around him, clinching him tightly like somebody might a long-lost son. The joy of his safe return clearly showing on her face.

'Angelo, you're safe,' she kept repeating incessantly. Tears ran down her face. Giuseppe and I were also full of relief. Angelo seemed almost unperturbed; his face expressionless. He'd been missing for more than three days and suddenly reappeared, almost back from the dead, we might have expected his face to be more animated.

Following the cries of joy from his return there were inevitable questions and some doubts. Why had those who had meticulously searched the forest been unable to locate him? After the furore of his dramatic reappearance had died down, he explained he had tried to keep up with Giuseppe and me but had lost his footing and had slid down a steep bank, where upon he banged his head on a tree stump. He had presumed his chances of survival were limited. Soon he was drifting in and out of consciousness.

His story then took a dramatic turn, when he told us that on one occasion, he regained consciousness and became aware of a beautiful woman peering over him, with blindingly bright radiant clothes. He told us he immediately felt a sense of tranquillity and any pains he had quickly disappeared. He could not move or even try to communicate with her, he was totally transfixed. She gently touched his head wound and the blood stopped seeping out. He closed his eyes briefly and she was gone. He felt strength in his body, like strength he had never felt before, after three days of lying motionless, he now had the impetus to make his way up the steep bank that he had slid down.

He found food in the forest to eat, mostly berries and clovers and other leaves. How he managed to find his way back, without a map, having no idea of the forest and its meandering paths, remains a mystery even to this day. He said it was an *inner force* that directed him.

My mother suggested he should try to retrace his steps at some point, to find the spot where the vision of the woman had appeared, that perhaps it was some kind of *holy shrine*, but he told her he did not wish to cause a stir, he'd had a spiritual experience, but he wanted it to be shrouded from the outside world, to keep it to himself.

Giuseppe and I had our doubts about Angelo's story. As I said before, Giuseppe knew the forest well and had been there many times, accompanied by people who had enlightened him as to its orientation and I had equally made several visits. Angelo on the other hand had been on his first foray and had managed to find his way back, without any kind of guidance. What had really happened during those three unaccounted days, was in our opinion, open to conjecture.

Angelo, obviously exhausted, went to bed. Giuseppe and I were sharing the next-door room. We became aware of Angelo muttering, but in some strange language we were not familiar with. His sleep seemed restless, and we were disturbed greatly by his strange discourse, that seemed to be like some kind of divine language.

The next day his parents arrived to take him home. There was relief all round. From our part it had proved an unnerving time. As time passed, we rarely saw Angelo, he was our cousin, but we were not close, despite living nearby. Giuseppe passed easily into a military academy to start his military training.

A year later I followed suit, to the same academy. Mother often sent us letters which included family news. It was little surprise when we learned that Angelo had decided to become a priest and was due to enter a seminary school.

Apparently since the *incident* there had been some marked changes. He'd grown stronger and didn't have the many health issues that had blighted much of his childhood. He was going to get some teaching experience, which is where he encountered you. On a weekend's leave we went to Angelo's eighteenth birthday party.

It was a drab and sober affair, mostly there were family members. Angelo, as ever, was hard to talk to and the only significant conversation was his entrance into seminary school.

Giuseppe and I willed the evening to come to a fast conclusion, we were far more used to boisterous military parties. At the end of the evening Angelo thanked us for coming and shook us both by the hand. There was no warmth between us, the shadow of the *incident* still hung over us.

"What a story,' I said to the young military officer, adding, 'and now Angelo is conducting wedding ceremonies for the nobility'."

"That is due to an uncle of mine, Cardinal Pietro Montilivio who made sure his diocese was appropriate to his social standing, I don't think Angelo would have appreciated getting his hands dirty rummaging around poor people."

"But he doesn't seem that comfortable being among those who are rich" I said, lifting my shoulders to emphasize my remark.

The military man frowned. "Angelo is a strange person and always was, let's talk more about you, you came with your parents, and there doesn't seem to be a man in your life, am I right?"

"You seem well informed," I retorted, evading his powerful gaze.

CHAPTER 21

An Invitation.

I had arrived at the wedding with an absurd fixation on a young priest I had barely spoken to. Now I was being pursued by a military man, who exuded confidence and in many ways was far more promising than the priest, who was extensively forbidden fruit.

"It is the regimental ball in two weeks," said the young officer, "and I would very much like you to join me for the occasion."

"We hardly know one another," I said adding, "I am sure you have many young female admirers, who would be far more suitable than me."

"None of them are as beautiful as you" he said, his eyes gleaming.

"I suppose I should refuse your invitation," I said, trying to give the air of being insouciant, "but I imagine I will be in respectable company."

"Of course," he replied, "I shall send a carriage to collect you." I was not sure what to make of this unexpected newcomer in my life. He was not as handsome as Angelo, but he was still very attractive to me, his uniform flawless.

He bowed punctiliously and clicked his shiny military boots together, as if he had just completed a mission and went off to engage with other guests. I went off in search of my parents, who had watched me, and the military man liaising and seemed happy about our union.

Father had consumed too much Prosecco and mother was wary he might be on the verge of making a fool of himself. Thankfully it was now the time for the speeches.

The military man, my new admirer, gave a rousing speech, which was well appreciated. I noticed Angelo at the back of the hall, looking on as an outsider, his face impassive. He did raise his glass of wine to toast the couple, but only out of politesse.

The wedding ended and guests began to disperse. Long before Angelo had drifted away, his exit no doubt unnoticed by many, I left by carriage with my parents. I caught sight of the young officer, leading a young girl to the dance floor, she seemed enraptured by him.

CHAPTER 22

The Regimental Party.

I took time to consider what to wear for the regimental ball. I bought a flamboyant silk dress with a pink silk mantle, as well as accessories, such as a handkerchief, and a fan, and some embroidered silk shoes, which I thought would be appropriate for the occasion.

The day of the ball arrived, and I spent some time with my maid perfecting my appearance. The carriage arrived exactly on time to take me to the regimental barracks, where the ball was to take place. I made my way out of the carriage, up some red carpeted steps, into the regimental headquarters. I joined those waiting to join the receiving line.

My name was announced. I was then required to shake hands with numerous officers along the line, with brief introductions. I caught sight of Lucius, like the other officers, in perfect attire, a light blue sash over his right shoulder. When I got to speak to him, he clicked his heels and bowed.

"It is wonderful to see you" he said, proceeding to talk in a typical military tone, firstly we will have some dinner, there will be some formal ceremony and then dancing will commence, would you care for an appetizer?"

I accepted his invitation for the drink, I was feeling slightly in awe of all the proceedings. A string quartet played some background music. The paintings on the walls were of scenes of battles. There were some bronze busts of generals who had served the regiment with distinction.

After we had finished our drinks, he led me arm in arm to where we would be dining. I was placed to the right of him, my name was written in elegant writing on a place card. I was placed next to Lucius and a rather aged major who was with his wife, both of whom had little to say, apart from matters to do with the regiment. I engaged mostly in conversation with Lucius who, as with our previous encounter, was brimming with confidence.

During the meal, there was the entrance and exit of the colours as well as various formal toasts and speeches, which seemed to be about boosting the morale of the regiment and recounting past glories. After the formal part of the evening had concluded, the dancing began. This added a far lighter note to the evening. Most of the older officers trooped off with their wives or watched as the younger officers and their partners danced with vigour.

Lucius once again proved to be an adept dancer. During a break in the proceedings, he suggested we might go for a walk on the lawn to get some fresh air. There were a few other couples scattered about, and it seemed a satisfactory thing to do.

"I hope you have enjoyed the evening so far" said Lucius, as we walked to rather secluded spot in the large garden that surrounded the regimental headquarters.

"It's been pleasant up to now," I replied, offering him a teasing smile.

Suddenly Lucius pulled me towards him and kissed me on the lips. He'd obviously had this in mind during the course of the evening. I hadn't anticipated this, but I found myself reciprocating readily. We stayed in a tight embrace for a long time before returning to the dancehall. He escorted me to a carriage that drove me home, after one, parting, with a rather decorous kiss.

CHAPTER 23

The Engagement.

From this point on we exchanged letters and had the odd liaisons between his military engagements. It wasn't long before he proposed to me. I accepted, feeling compelled to do so, despite some reservations, particularly about being an officer's wife in the insular stuffy barracks. Lucius wasn't exactly the vision I'd had for a husband, I'd never been exactly sure what I wanted, apart from my yearning for Angelo.

Both families were naturally delighted with the news, when we made our announcement. Various social events were organized before the wedding to celebrate our engagement. The wedding took a lot of organization, the guest list was full of noblemen and dignitaries and inevitably various military men, along with their wives.

My parents and Lucius seemed to be the ones who dictated how the wedding would be, while I appeared to drift into the background, neither consulted or involved apart from the requisites of wedding dress fittings.

As the day drew ever closer, I began to bore of the whole procedure. By contrast Lucius seemed to gain in eagerness and excitement. Lucius' uncle presided over the ceremony with Angelo assisting, (Lucius' mother had insisted). We exchanged brief words with Angelo, who offered us his congratulations. The wedding reception was a rousing event; a lavish spread of food was devoured, followed by energetic dancing.

Lucius and I left the proceedings through a guard of honour and set off on a memorable honeymoon. After two weeks we returned to our new home provided by the regiment. Life seemed idyllic. However soon our married life started to be marked by absences when Lucius was forced to go away on various missions. Inevitably we began talking about starting a family, which we imagined would make our life complete.

CHAPTER 24

An Empty Marriage.

After several months, which turned into years I began to become anxious that an offspring was not forthcoming. As time moved on my concerns grew even stronger. My sisters had become pregnant without a problem, relatively shortly after their marriages. Mother and father began to dwell on the point that I had not provided Lucius with an heir. An unimagined burden began to creep into our relationship.

Lucius began spending more time with his regimental friends, leaving me on my own. He would return home after a long drinking spree, slump on the canapé and sometimes didn't even make it to the marital bed. There seemed no obvious solution to this complication.

His brother, Giuseppe who he seemed to have spent most of his life trying equal, already had two children, a boy and a girl and another on the way. The regiment was brimming with children, but not in our household.

During the course of a long hot summer Lucius was sent on a mission that would take three weeks or indeed much longer. I was not given any information as to what this mission might involve or where he would be. He said goodbye with a brisk kiss on my cheeks, telling me not to worry.

I had little much to do, I spent my time reading, or going for walks by the lake in the grounds of the barracks. I was feeling increasingly isolated. The other wives I found to be boring, with little conversation, apart from family matters, their children, and regimental tittle tattle.

CHAPTER 25

An Appearance of an Old Acquaintance.

While setting off on my walk, I suddenly came across a familiar face. It was somebody who was entrenched in my past. Angelo walked up to me and his soft voice, said "Lucrezia, how are you?"

I was surprised he had remembered my name, let alone make the effort to approach me.

"Father Angelo, I'm fine, what brings you here?"

"I am filling in for Father Piero, who has gone for a retreat, he asked me to help some children who are preparing for their first communion."

"I see," I replied.

"So where is Lucius, on some mission I imagine?" demanded Angelo.

"Yes, he's away, as it happens, I responded, will be back in a couple of weeks. I'm going for a walk by the lake, perhaps you might care to join me."

Father Angelo weighed up my offer. "I was going to a local hospital to visit the sick, but as it is such a fine day, I would be happy to accompany you," said Angelo accepting my invitation.

We walked rather ponderously side by side, each finding it hard to strike up some kind of rapport. I rather regretted asking him to join me, but I had spent too many long periods alone. I was hungry for company, any kind of company.

As we approached the lake, he suddenly yelped in pain.

"What's the matter?" I demanded urgently.

"I have something in my foot," he said grimacing. He

sat down and took off his sandal, his face contorted in pain.

He had walked on some broken glass, probably the result of some children who'd broken a wine bottle by throwing stones at it.

"I suggest we go to the boat house, there could be something to help, going back to my house is now much further." I had been to the boat house which was situated on a small island. Lucius and I had a picnic there. I seemed to recall there was a box with some basic medical provisions. There would most likely be the occasional injury sustained by those fishing on the lake.

I suggested he put his arm on my shoulder in order that I help to support his weight. He hobbled with my help over to a rowing boat. I rowed us over to the boat house and opened the door and helped him over to a dusty canopy.

I had scant medical knowledge, but I surmised it was necessary to clean the wound. Opening the medical box, I found a needle and some tweezers. It caused Angelo a lot of pain, but I managed to extract the offending piece of glass. I found some bandages and wrapped them gently around his foot.

Scouting about the boat house, I discovered a bottle of whisky, which had been left for the pleasure of those profiting from the boat house.

"Would you like a glass, it might help you take your mind off the pain," I suggested. Reticent at first, he finally accepted my offer, and I poured out two glasses. It seemed like we would remain a while in the boat house, while the pain eased off.

Conversation between us flowed much more easily than it had in previous encounters. Maybe because we had made some physical contact, or because I had helped to alleviate a painful situation, he connected with me. Perhaps he trusted me now. As a boy he had suffered abuse, due to his frailty, he had little faith in humanity, which was why he had chosen to take refuge by being priest.

What still intrigued me about him was the story Lucius had related, his *missing* days. I imagined if I gently probed him, he might just tell me the truth. After a moment's silence, I suddenly perked up and posed the question.

CHAPTER 26

The Story Retold.

"Lucius told me that you went missing for three days, had some kind of vision and miraculously returned, ever stronger, is that right?"

He went silent for a while and seemed deeply pensive. Perhaps he wanted to release the truth, after containing it for so long. Or maybe he did indeed trust me, for some reason. We were secluded on this small island, and in some ways, it was an intimate moment, between the two of us. Finally, he spoke.

"I was still a boy at the time, and boys have wild imaginations. If you want me to tell you the truth, I will, but never tell another soul, not even your husband." I assured him I would guard any secrets he wished to disclose and keep them strictly to myself. He seemed to be reassured.

He began to relate his story. "I was a fool to choose to join both Giuseppe and Lucius, in the first place. I suppose I wanted to try to prove to be their equal, but I could never be like them. Lucius, from an early age, always looked up to his older brother and together they were always a formidable close pair.

I suppose I was always in awe of them, myself a sickly child, while they were active, fearless, full of life, exuding confidence and with a taste for adventure. My life had always been sheltered. My mother was evidently overprotective, and this was heightened because of my regular ailments.

I had begged Mother to let me stay with my cousins, while they went on a short trip abroad. I soon realized I was a figure of fun in the eyes of Giuseppe and Lucius. They wanted to make capital out of my frailty, with scant regard for kinship.

As we made progress on our hunting trip, I soon became aware of my limitations and found it hard to keep up with the other two, who were hardy and accustomed to such conditions. They indulged in cruel tricks to make me feel constantly on edge. I had never been camping before. Mother thought it inappropriate for a child of my fragile disposition. Equally I had never been hunting, I was not inclined towards killing an animal, but perhaps I had an arbitrary curiosity to witness a kill.

With the heat and flies buzzing around me, and the distant laughter of Giuseppe and Lucius, I laboured my way through undergrowth until we reached the camp. Giuseppe and Lucius continued to delight in the childish pranks, which I begrudgingly yielded to. I even had the indignity of being pushed into a malodorous pond.

Being accustomed to city life, I found the countryside an austere environment and nature appeared to be my foe. The two brothers were well acquainted with the quirks of nature and knew their way round the forest and how to live off it and survive in rugged conditions. The two boys tried to flaunt their adultness, by drinking wine and cajoling me into drinking, something I had never done.

On the first night I hardly slept, I missed the comforts of a proper bed. I heard the distant sounds of nocturnal animals calling out, the forest was alive with a clamour of sound. I could never have anticipated what was to follow. The next day as the others set off fishing, I spent the day mostly on my own, I took the opportunity to read a book.

Boredom sunk in and I decided to take a walk on my own, while being careful to remember my way back to the camp. After a while I heard movement in front of me through the undergrowth.

At first, I thought it might be an animal, perhaps a deer or even a wild boar, the prey which Giuseppe and Lucius often talked about, during his hunting exploits. On closer inspection I saw a man with long wild hair and a beard moving timidly through the thicket. I felt confident he hadn't seen me, and I began to covertly follow him.

Sometimes he would stop and rummage around some bushes, picking foliage, placing clumps of leaves into a worn-out bag. When he had attained what he was looking for, he would move on. I had never seen a man like him, I was fascinated by him.

I followed him until he descended a steep grassy bank, gripping a rope. I was able to catch sight of his simple habitat. It was next to small stream and was covered by wild vegetation. He had fabricated this house with branches. It was well hidden from any outsiders. I could see a fire he had made earlier which had nearly burnt out, next to the fire were some pots, he used for cooking. He was obviously totally self-sufficient. I heard him vaguely muttering to himself. I could not understand a word. I decided to leave him and returned to the camp. Giuseppe and Lucius were still not back, so I went back to reading my book, still pondering my discovery.

The two brothers returned, excited about the night-time hunting escapade which was soon to come. We prepared a meal and then they busied themselves with preparation for the hunt. We set off as darkness began to set in.

We had barely walked very far when the storm began. It was like no storm I had ever experienced before. There was only one option to shelter from the storm, back in our camp. Giuseppe and Lucius made progress, while I struggled as the terrain became more and more perilous. After a while I lost sight of them. I arrived at the same place where I had seen the man in his den and instinctively slid down the slippery bank, letting myself down slowly by holding onto the rope.

The old man was huddled inside and was shocked to discover he was not alone and had an unexpected interloper. His reaction to my sudden arrival, once his surprise had abated, was one of joy. It was clear that with his confused mind he was mistaking me for somebody else who was significant to him. He kept repeating 'you have returned'.

'I don't really know you,' I tried to contradict him. His enthusiasm was strong, it was like his spirit had been lifted. The storm continued and branches and debris began to slide down the bank camouflaging his secret lair even more. Had I done the right thing? I seemed to be harbouring from a storm with a crazy man. My clothes were soaked through, and I began to shiver. He found some dry blankets which he draped over me. When he got a closer look at me his face changed, and his exuberance seemed to diminish.

'You are not him,' he repeated repeatedly, wiping away some tears that had welled up in his eyes. Neither of us slept during the night, nor spoke to one another.

'Why are you here?' he demanded the next morning.

'I was with my cousins, we got split up, due to the storm,' I explained. I told him I was staying with my cousins, who were embarking on a hunting expedition.

'Guns,' he exclaimed. 'Yes, I replied they had guns.'

The word *gun* seemed to disturb him greatly. After I had explained myself, I dared to ask him about his story.

It turned out his story was a tragic one. He explained he had a family and worked on the estate of a rich Count. His life was good, he loved his wife and family. He lived in a cottage and tended the estate's woods and the game that populated it.

When his son was seventeen, he had decided to take him on a weekend hunting trip for deer and wild boar. What he didn't realize was that a younger brother stealthily followed them. The two brothers were close, and the younger one had been disappointed to be left out on this trip.

Tragedy struck when the father heard some rustling of leaves and presumed there was a deer about to leave the thicket. He fired his gun and went over to the bushes, only to discover his second son dead, a bullet had lodged in his skull. He died in his father's arms almost instantaneously. The father sent his oldest son back to the cottage. Looking at his dead son, while cradling him in his arms, made him conclude that he couldn't face anybody. He left his dead son and began walking and walking, non-stop for days and days on end. Finally, he arrived at the forest, where he was to make his home. Of course, he felt double guilt, for killing one of his own children, but also for deserting his wife and family, who would have to fend for themselves.

Each day he would dwell on that terrible day. He was wary of any people who ventured through the forest. He lived in constant fear of being discovered and having to face the world, condemned for doing a heinous act. When I had suddenly intruded upon his world, his befuddled mind had presumed I was his son. He had not spoken to a soul in years. He lived off the forest, which not only provided for his needs in food, but also, when necessary for medicine. He seemed of perfectly good health, despite living in rugged conditions.

He told me to stay put as he went off to forage for food. He came back with a bag full of dandelions, elderberries, clovers, wild grape vine as well as an assortment of other leaves and berries. He made us a kind of tea, made from rose hips which helped to warm me up. The storm had long since died down and was now a memory. I thought about the brothers, desperate to find me, surely going through hell, in their anguish, I didn't really care, I was enjoying being away from the world I was familiar with, as well as being cooped up with a man, who had escaped from the world.

I was in no hurry to leave and re-join the outside world, the psychological antagonism I was accustomed to with Giuseppe and Lucius and the over pampering of my mother.

Most of the day was spent talking to the old man. Later in the day we heard voices, and dogs barking. I was sure there would many people looking for me by now, my disappearance must have a caused a big furore. The old man assured me the dogs would not be able to detect us and would not venture down the steep incline. Of course, he put out the fire he had used to cook us food. It was true the men and dogs passed us by. There was the worry that the men might return, but hopefully as they had searched the area close to the old man's hideout and having found no signs of me, they would centre their attention elsewhere.

As darkness surrounded the forest the old man went about searching for food. Again, he came back with plenty. The forest was bountiful, and surprisingly I seemed to benefit from it and gain strength. Over time the old man had become enlightened about the properties of plants. It soon became clear in my head that I would at some point, have to re-enter the world I was more familiar with. The old man did indeed mention that it was inappropriate for a person of my standing to stay living in such conditions and that I should not desert those who held me dear, like my parents.

My time spent with the old man was enlightening. He told, me despite the cruel fate which had devastated his life, he was still a strong believer in God. Indeed, his parting words were "spread the word of God". It was strange mounting the steep bank for the last time.

The old man was able to direct me back to the house. When we reached a point whereby, I could find my own way back, we parted. I could see much sadness in his eyes. Equally I was sad to leave him, to a life that would be forever in solitude. When I was discovered by a servant, my reappearance was met with great surprise. I made up a totally different version as to what had happened and had sworn, I would not give away the man's whereabouts.

As time passed, I set my heart on being a priest. It seemed a natural progression to give my life to God. In a way my life took a new direction following this encounter with this old man. In many ways he emboldened me. I decided this new vigour I had attained would be best engaged as a life of a priest.

I felt sure that under the auspices of being a priest I would be protected from a world I had long feared, it offered the perfect form of escapism. I would gain respect which I felt I had long been denied. My life would be preordained; I would not have to follow a career in pursuit of money. I would be beyond reproach, as I would be deemed as a man who had decided to devote his life to God. Being a priest tied in well with my character. I was never going to be the life and soul of a party. Many would say I am rather sober in character, the perfect credentials for the priesthood.

"But what about having a family," I cut in, "you must have considered this"?

"Apart from my mother," replied the priest with a sigh, "I have never really paid much attention to women."

"Not even when you were surrounded by young girls at the school, hankering after you? I am sure you must have felt this, priests are human after all, or am I wrong?"

CHAPTER 27

A Shocking Turn of Events.

He seemed to be irritated by my comment. His mood changed in an instant. It was like I was in contact with a totally new man for the first time. I had unravelled a darker side of his character. He glared at me intently.
"Who are you to make such presumptions," the priest said, with a snarl, "what is this fascination some women have concerning the susceptibility of priests to desires of the flesh?"
"I am sorry," I said meekly, "I didn't want to embarrass you." He glared at me, baring his teeth. His body was shaking with rage.
"I suppose you think I am inadequate as a man; I imagine you think I am an impotent shell of a man."
Without warning he lunged towards me and smothered me with his weight. This seemingly chaste man who I had seen as being totally effete in spirit had somehow been roused. He was forcing himself on me. The shock was too much for me. I thrashed about with little effect, trying to release myself.
"Let me go," I managed to say in as strong a voice I could summon up.
"You think I am blind to your coquetry," he snarled, "I was aware of you from the start, you led me here, you want this to happen, don't you! You married a man, my cousin, so you could still retain contact with me."
What he said was not exactly the truth, but I couldn't deny that there was some authenticity in his words, I had long had impure thoughts about him, but I never anticipated events would evolve in such a tempestuous

way.
With one free hand he began to manoeuvre his cassock upwards, while pulling his underclothes downward, while keeping me pinioned to the floor. Once he had succeeded in this task, he proceeded to violently lift up my dress and displace my underclothes.
"Stop this, in God's name stop!" I shrieked. My words were futile, things had moved on so quickly, he was now a man possessed.
He entered inside me and began to thrust himself with fervour. With a sigh he reached his climax and rested momentarily to recapture his poise. He then stood up and rearranged his clothes and ambled to the doorway, without saying a word.

CHAPTER 28

A Mortal Blow.

Suddenly I felt this uncontrollable surge of anger, as if a powerful unstoppable force was driving me on. The storm had cleared away and he seemed to be looking over the lake that was now bathed in golden sunlight. He was so absorbed in his thoughts. It allowed me time to find a filleting knife, among some fishing equipment.

Moving with great rapidity I lunged towards him, jabbing the knife into his back, while letting out a raucous cry. He jerked forward and fell into the water, with a great ripple being discharged. My anger was unabated I leaned over and thrust the knife viciously many times, in the back of his neck, all down his spine, his crimson blood spewing into the murky water of the lake forming a crimson plume of priest's blood.

His body was now limp and lifeless, I had satisfied my desire for retribution. Momentarily I stared at this body still gushing blood, but bobbing gently in the water, face down.

I realized if I left him close to the boat house, his body would be quickly discovered and that I needed to submerge it in a far deeper part of the lake. I found a hefty anchor resting in the boathouse and put it in the rowing boat. I dragged the dead priest from the water and managed with great effort to manoeuvre him onto the rowing boat.

When I felt the water was sufficiently deep enough, with some chord I attached the anchor around the torso of the lifeless priest. I pushed him over the side of the boat, then managed to push his body out of the boat and with an oar direct it down to the bottom of the lake. Soon he was engulfed in the dingy water. I was now alone. Tears ran down my cheeks. I held my head and my hands and wailed in agony.

I rowed back to the boathouse to get everything back to how it was, despite my tormented mind I meticulously left no evidence that any crime had taken place. I cleaned away any traces of blood and placed the knife where I had found it. The only missing object would be the anchor, but who would miss a rusty old anchor that served little purpose? To my horror I noticed I had some spattering of the priest's blood on my frock. I found an old rag, dunked it in water and tried to scrub it away.

Satisfied with my endeavours, as the light began to fade, I rowed back to the shore, hoping that nobody had spotted me dispatching the priest into a watery grave. Wearily I walked back to my house. Occasionally I heard muffled voices, but I evaded any contact with anybody. I opened the door of the house, sat down on the sofa and just stared into space, still unable to believe what had happened. I couldn't sleep, in my head I was still stabbing the back of the priest, my hatred for him after what he had done was resonating without appease.

Lucius was not due back for a while, his mission incomplete, which gave me time to gather my thoughts.

Should I tell him what had happened? I dismissed this idea immediately. He would never understand, how could I expect him to? He might jump to conclusions, think that I had led the priest on, that I was to blame as to what had happened. Moreover, he would see me as a murderer; I had slain a man, his cousin, a priest no less. He would be duty bound to report my crime to the authorities. A murder of this kind carried a heavy punishment, that of death.

Despite the strong burden of what had occurred, I still felt that I was still young and that my life still served some kind of purpose, but what direction it would take from here on, I couldn't determine.

I spent days without sleep, barely eating, never leaving the house, not speaking to a soul, just trapped in my own bleak thoughts, my mind a living hell. I closed the curtains of my house, as if I was away, so nobody would bother me. Occasionally I heard voices getting closer to the house, I willed the people to leave, not enter my repressive existence.

The pain and horror would never leave me, however hard I endeavoured to cast it out of my mind. I knew I had to start to regain my composure, time was passing, and Lucius might return at any moment, I never could tell when his missions were completed, to find me in this state of utter despair. It took all my mental strength to dress and open the curtains of the house. Feeling extremely weak, I forced myself to eat and spent some time in the bathroom, applying makeup. Looking in the mirror, I had never seen myself so haggard. I cried and cried without cessation. My face looked pallid.

CHAPTER 29

Facing the Outside World.

For my next test I needed to open my front door and step outside into daylight. I walked slowly downstairs and timidly began to unlock the door. I walked out of what had been my refuge from the outside world. There were soldiers milling about and the odd spouse going about some chores, the barracks was bustling as ever. I walked but with no destination in mind, I just wanted to see if I could reunite with some kind of reality. One of the officer's wives passed me, offering a cheery "hello". I forced a limp smile, but no words passed my lips. Despite this, in a way I felt like I had broken through a boundary at least.

I approached the barracks' chapel. I became aware of some music and singing. I should have headed off in another direction, but I wasn't as alert as I might normally be. Suddenly the doors of the church flew open. A young officer, who I was vaguely acquainted with, stepped out with his bride, both with beaming smiles. The congregation, many in military attire, swept out of the church, laughing, and smiling and scattering rice over the couple.

I was comfortable with what I was looking at, until out stepped a priest. I had to double check, he was the same height, build, had similar hair and facial features to Father Angelo Amentini, in my deranged state I couldn't differentiate the two. He looked awkward, so young and fresh faced, he must have recently left seminary school. Just looking at him sent spasms of fear, hatred, and disgust. I vomited. Somebody saw my distress. "Are you alright?" a woman asked in a kindly voice.

I was trying to regain my composure. The pungent smell of the vomit added to my discomfort. The woman gently put a hand on my shoulder, as a form of comfort. I didn't speak to her, I couldn't, I batted her away, as if she was an unwanted intrusion. I began to run back in the direction of my house, but as I was running, I felt my legs give way and I collapsed in a heap.

Despite the church congregation being enraptured, following the completion of a joyous marriage ceremony, many gasped as they caught sight of me strewn on the ground. The woman who had tried to aid me, shouted for help. A doctor was summoned. I was placed on a stretcher and taken to the barracks' infirmary.

A doctor examined and tried to question me. I never answered him, I just lay on the bed, comatose, staring at the ceiling. It was necessary for me to stay in the hospital under surveillance. I would have protested this, but I felt so weak and debilitated. The doctor gave strict instructions to build up my strength to get me to eat, having concluded one of my foremost problems was lack of nourishment.

At first I resisted any aid, when a stern army matron tried to coax me into eating a soup, I thrashed out at her, scattering soup all over the floor. She scolded me fiercely, as might a mother with an uncooperative petulant child. Later a young nurse with a softer approach was sent to get me to eat. This time I relented and hesitantly supped the soup.

My first night at the hospital was agitated. I drifted in and out of sleep. Occasionally I woke up, there were cries of pain from other patients. At one point I heard the cries of a woman, who I perceived was going into labour. There were the cries of soldiers who has sustained injuries. I even heard one young man call out for his mother. The hospital was simply a cacophony of noise.

And what of Angelo Amentini? Was his soul where it belonged, in hell? Was his permanent absence now common knowledge? Were there once again search parties scouring the local surroundings in search of the stray priest? I doubted a body had been found, it would be by now decomposing, covered in algae and vegetation. Grotesque visions appeared in my head.

I cried out. A young nurse came rushing to my aid, she found me muttering indecipherable words, my body convulsing uncontrollably, my face appearing to relive some momentous horrific crisis.

"Calm yourself," she said in a desperate attempt to comfort me. I couldn't focus on her, she was like a spectre, creeping into my consciousness. The nurse repeated herself several times, each repetition growing in intensity, as she tried to contain my state of anguish. When I had finally regained my composure, I clutched onto her, pressing my face into her chest, my breathing intense. She put her two arms around me and held me gently, rocking gently, like a mother becalming a tearful child. I have no idea how long she devoted herself to settling me down. When she began to detach herself from our tight clench, in a weak barely audible voice I begged her not to leave me.

She gently manoeuvred me down, my head resting on a pillow. She rearranged my bed sheets.

She stood over me and said, "you seem to have gone through a great ordeal, why don't you tell me about it, whatever you say will remain totally confidential."

Judging by the short time we had spent with one another, the nurse seemed a woman with a kind heart, but under no circumstances could I tell a living a soul, on this matter I was totally resolute. I would have to carry this burden for the rest of my living days.

How could I respond to her? My mind worked quickly. Finally, I said in a feeble unconvincing voice.

"I am fine now, please leave me."

"I have my duties to attend to, but if you need me, I will be close at hand," said the nurse as she glided out of my room, no doubt with a perplexed mind, after what she had witnessed.

It took time for me to drift back to sleep. Monotonous days followed, as the hospital tried to rebuild my strength. One morning I was still in a lethargic state when I heard footsteps gaining momentum to my room. I wondered if Lucius had returned. I had sporadically thought about him. I was somewhat dreading seeing him, I would have the burden of guilt, every time our eyes connected. There would be so many lies I would have to concoct. Our relationship had been fraught over a period of time, our inability to conceive a child had compounded our disharmony.

It was not Lucius who entered the room, but the young priest who had officiated the regimental marriage, I had witnessed before my breakdown.

He smiled at me. "I am on my rounds to offer some comfort" said the young priest, in a soft voice that was all too similar to Angelo's dulcet voice, still beaming a radiant smile. I stared at him, as If my body had turned totally rigid. Despite my lack of response, he continued in the manner expected of a priest among sick people.

"I am here to offer God's comfort during your time of affliction, I am here to pass on God's love to the sick."

A voice screamed in my head.

"But your God has forsaken me!"

The young priest must have noticed my reticence to communicate, my awkwardness must have been clearly visible on my face. I imagined that he would be well received wherever he went, especially by those whose lives were ebbing away or those of ill health who needed spiritual guidance to help to sustain them. A young handsome man with a fresh face would surely light up even a drab infirmary.

"Who are you?" I demanded, looking with disdain.

"My name is Father Rosario Caruso, I am replacing Father Piero, who sadly is confined to this infirmary, having been taken seriously sick following a sudden illness during a retreat."

"I see" I replied with little conviction.

Then without thinking I said, "I thought Father Angelo often came here to do things on Father Piero's behalf."

The young priest's voice dropped to almost a whisper.

"Sadly, Father Angelo has been absent for a number of days, we hope he will be back with us soon."

"Oh, I see," I said trying to exude some kind of air of surprise.

Maybe his absence had been attributed to doubts about his priest's calling, I thought to myself. I tried to ascertain the young priest's position concerning this possibility.

"Perhaps Father Angelo has abandoned the priesthood," I said with a pondering voice and a vague smile. The young priest looked at me with critical eyes, his body seemed to tense up.

"Father Angelo, abandon the priesthood! Renounce his holy orders! He would never leave his flock."

"Did you know him well?" I solicited. The young

priest's voice dropped.

"Well, I have to admit, we only met a couple of times, but Father Angelo was known for his absolute devotion to the clergy and his unequivocal belief in God." I wondered whether the young priest fully believed all that he was trying to convey to me. I thrust the matter further.

"He is like you, young, maybe susceptible to doubts, perhaps his reputation is spurious, it always hard to really delve deep into the mind of another person, even a priest."

"I don't like what you are implying," said the priest his previous composure waning, adding unconvincingly after a deep sigh, "I am sure there is a simple explanation for Father Angelo's absence, and he will be back with his flock in the near future."

"I hope so Father," I said deceitfully. "And what of you?" asked the priest, "why are you here?"

"The doctors tell me I am undernourished; hopefully I should be out of here very soon."

"I see," said the priest, nodding his head gently, perhaps deeming I was one of milder afflicted patients he'd come across on his rounds.

"Perhaps you would like to take the holy sacrament of communion?" ventured the young priest. In his hand there was a velvet sachet with a cross motif on it. He held an expectant smile, as if he was offering me an opportunity that under no circumstances could be declined.

When I refused by simply saying "I'd prefer not to." his facial expression changed to one of utter dismay, followed by a look of utter indignation.

"Are you a church goer?" he asked, his eyes probing me with an inquisitor's stare.

"I have gone to church all of my life, I spent time in a nunnery, I still accompany my husband each week to the regimental chapel," I replied flatly.

"Then why would you not wish to take the holy sacraments, especially at a time you are of ill health?" demanded the priest, still confounded by my behaviour.

"What do you think you are offering me, some kind of magic potion?" I said sardonically, with a semblance of a sarcastic smile.

"I am offering you the body of Christ, he who died on the cross for all our sins," replied Father Rosario resolutely.

"I am more than familiar with the teachings of the church, they were enforced on me from an early age, anything you say to me, will be something I have heard many times, from the pulpits of churches, from the mouths of sanctimonious priests. You come here to impose your beliefs on the sick and the vulnerable. I imagine most of them welcome you, they are easy prey and clearly you are a handsome man who must appear like a beacon of hope among all those who have little left on their lives or will suffer the pain of their injuries for the rest of their lives. However, a morsel of unleavened wheat bread is not going to make my life any different or take me closer to this God, you fervently believe in."

He shook his head, "You seem to have totally lost your faith" the priest said mournfully, adding "your heart seems filled with loathing, how can this be so?".

I replied, gently nodding, "it is true that I carry a heavy burden in my heart, but my pain will not wane through the rhetoric of a priest."

"Would you not like to make a confession, to rid yourself of this burden you carry?" asked the priest, he held out his hands as if offering an invisible gift, "wouldn't you wish to be at one with God?"

"You don't seem to listen to me Father," I replied frostily, "you have nothing to give me, apart from emboldening my pain and trying to impose your will on me, your very presence in this room disturbs me greatly."

The young priest was unmoved.

"A confession helps to heal the soul and the holy Eucharist is spiritual food that takes you closer to God," the young priest attested.

"But what if your God doesn't exist, or if it does is a cruel and malicious one?" I said without qualms.

"God is always good, and Jesus looked after his flock," the young priest pontificated. "As for his existence, we need to welcome God into our hearts," said the young priest, pointing an admonitory finger at me. "He is everywhere and those who don't believe will be sent to the fires of hell." He seemed horrified I had called his being into question. "Hell! I yelled, doubtlessly disturbing anyone in earshot, there is hell on this earth, wars, pestilence, poverty, disease, all of which are as prevalent as this God you believe in!"

"Your words are blasphemous and untrue," scowled the young priest, "God loves and protects his children and the things you mention are the works of the Devil, the very Devil that has the power to enchant disbelievers, a trap you seem to have fallen into."

Father Rosario seemed to have offered his final riposte and brusquely told me he had other patients to see on his rounds. He marched out of my room at speed, obviously perturbed by our brief and awkward encounter. I was angry with myself for engaging with him in such a way. I should have pretended to be too sick or drowsy and simply not bothered to converse with him.

It was my anger towards priests and beyond that God, that had overcome me. In a way our encounter had served a purpose, matters were clearer in my head, I had located the roots of my rancour, my life was on a new course now, which I would have no control over.

CHAPTER 30

Another Priest, More Anger to Deal With.

That night I was woken up a patient next door.

"Wine! I need wine!" a voice grumbled.

"It is not good for you Father, Doctor has told you many times, you have to drink in moderation or even better not at all," replied a female voice in a stern fashion.

"I don't care what this doctor said, what do doctors know anyway?"

"They know Father that you drink too much and have been brought here to our infirmary, for your own protection, you are not a well man," replied the voice of the nurse, the matron who had tried to nag me to eat.

Then suddenly I heard a shriek.

"Father Piero, restrain yourself Father!" said the matron in an indignant voice. I heard a cackling laugh; the old priest was delighting in his mischievous act. Presumably he'd succeeded in groping the heftily built nurse, no mean feat, I imagined, as she came across as a formidable woman.

I was discovering a side of Father Piero I could never have imagined. I had sat through his church services and had made some small talk with him, never any meaningful conversation, however such brief encounters told me he was an affable person. To me he was just another regular priest, without any foibles. He seemed well liked by all the officers and their wives and was often invited to social occasions. He presided over many ceremonies and was an intricate part of the fabric of the barracks' life. He must have carefully concealed his drinking escapades and maybe only a few people must have been aware of this hidden indiscretion.

His health issues became apparent to me the next day. I was party to a conversation between Father Piero and Father Rosario, who was once again doing his rounds. Father Rosario made a point of not visiting me. In a way it was a relief, as if he had provoked me once again. In my head we were now two bitter antagonists.

"How are you, Father Piero?" demanded the young priest, innocently.

"I feel a prisoner in this place, I want to leave," snapped the old priest.

"You know unfortunately this is not possible," replied Father Rosario.

"What do you mean?" demanded Father Piero bitterly.

"The doctors have tried to explain everything to you, over and over again, said the young priest in a fraught voice. Their prognostic is not good, you have a serious heart condition, you need to prepare yourself to meet the Almighty. I am sure he will take you to his bosom."

"Only the good lord knows when we are ready to depart this world, snarled the rancorous old man, adding doggedly, and the last thing I would wish for myself is to be confined to this sad infirmary, with a dogmatic bore like you."

"I am afraid you have little choice Father, said the youthful priest shaking his head, and I would suggest this is a perfect environment for you, one of serenity, a place that is perfect for contemplation and prayer."

"A place where a person is most likely to die of boredom," murmured the old man.

"I have brought you some books," piped up Father Rosario, trying to lighten the tone of the conversation.

The old priest read out loud the titles of the books, among them were St. Catherine of Padua's book on Purgatory, there was starkly titled, "Preparation for Death" and "Considerations on Eternal Truths" by Saint Alphonsus de Angelico. Each book was an unwanted pronouncement of his impending death.

He took the pile of books and flung them with all his might at the young priest, who recoiled in shock. I heard the young man yelp. Such exertion brought about a fit of wheezing and coughing in the old man. The young priest anxiously called for a nurse. It took a long time for the old man's wheezing outbreak to subside.

The nurse wondered whether the young priest Rosario had not said something to agitate the old man. She noted some books strewn on the floor.

"Maybe Father Piero shouldn't have too many visits, he needs time alone, plenty of rest, don't you think Father Rosario? said the nurse in an assertive manner.

The young priest seemed to meekly leave the nurse to deal with the old man who was clearly fighting to stay alive, closer to meeting his maker than he clearly wished.

I had to endure the old priest's interminable coughing. Couldn't he just hurry up and die? It was true he wasn't of the same ilk as Father Rosario, a zealous young priest eager to bludgeon the church's beliefs on populace and further its influence. Any positive thoughts I might have had for Father Piero were soon to be dispelled. Somehow, he must have become aware of my presence in the room next to his.

CHAPTER 31

Violation Again.

It must have been sometime in the middle of the night. I was in a deep sleep. Suddenly I was conscious of another person in my room, who was in the process of pulling off the blankets of my bed. I tried to scream, but a pudgy hand proceeded to smother my mouth and restrain any kind of plea for help.

"Don't do that my pretty," a voice said, before letting out a gentle cackle. I was becoming more awake as well as my fear mounting.

"I just want a little fiddle my pretty, nothing more, nothing less," the voice said.

I tried to struggle free, my assailant was bulky, and I was pinned down by his weight.

His free hand began to pull up my night dress. His putrid breath stank, I was forced to breathe it in through my nose. Someone had given him access to some alcohol, presumably wine, either this or had managed somehow to procure some.

Despite the obvious differences in physique my mind was drawn to thoughts of Father Angelo. It was as if he was assailing me once more, not the demented old priest, who had intruded my bed taking advantage of my vulnerability. The old degenerate managed attain his desire to grope me. I bit hard into his hand and managed to wrestle him off my bed. He began to violently cough, more so than ever before. Rather than being found in the room of another patient, particularly a married female patient, he managed to return to his own room and bed.

For a while I lay as if paralysed, trying to regain my

composure. What had happened was sickening. If I spoke to those in any kind of authority, I was sure the old rogue would get a telling off, excuses would be made on his behalf, the matter would be laid to rest. If I told Lucius, I imagined he would be angry, but would he seek revenge on a priest, a man of God, after all.

I felt bound to resolve this situation myself, in the same way I had with Father Angelo, but this time I felt I had to be more subtle in the way I would dispatch the old priest. I heard the voice of a nurse coming to the aid of the old priest. She offered him water, while he still carried on coughing and wheezing.

When I felt confident the nurse had well and truly left and the priest was on his own, stealthily I picked a pillow from my bed and crept quickly into the old priest's room unnoticed. I placed the pillow over the old man's face, who was unaware of my presence and his impending death. With all my strength I pressed down on his face. I had calculated it wouldn't take much to take this man's life, he was close to death as it was.

For a while he seemed to resist me and fought for breath, but soon his resistance began to ebb away. When I was sure I had completed the task, I had set out to do, I slipped back into my room. Satisfied I would not be bothered again by the depraved old priest, I managed to drift off into an agitated sleep.

The next morning, I woke up to the sound of concerned voices.

A voice kept repeating "Father Piero" over and over again. As he failed to respond, the voice began to become more and more insistent.

"He was drinking," a voice said.

"Somebody must have given him some alcohol, look there's a wine bottle," another voice said.

"He has no pulse; he must have died during the night," said an urgent voice.

Had I killed him? My mind was bleary, and memories were now decidedly remote. Had I imagined him entering my room, then violating me? My night had been so disturbed and my mind so delirious, particularly following my encounter with Father Angelo.

Whatever, I was comforted by the fact that he was dead. The shadow of his looming presence in my close proximity was now dispersed forever. This at least was a relief for me. I heard a long discourse between the nurses. A doctor would be required, the formalities needed to be addressed, including a death certificate; he would then be placed in a mortuary, then the chapel of rest.

There was no suspicion of foul play; the old man had simply died in his sleep. Perhaps it was a blessing to one and all. After all he had been a pest, he'd molested the matron and doubtlessly other nurses on the ward. He was a drunk, his demeanour repellent. A fraudulent debauched priest was simply no loss to the world and if such a place as hell exists, I was sure this was where he would reside. I listened to further conversations including the arrival of the doctor, who went about his duties before signing the death warrant. I heard as he was finally taken from his room on a trolley his corpse no doubt shrouded in a sheet. Now I really felt totally absent from him.

CHAPTER 32

A Terrible Realization.

Monotonous days passed, Lucius had been away over month, or was it more, I'd lost count of days and had no sense of time. I was confined in this bleak hospital almost a similar length of time to his absence, I knew that. But there was another matter I had on my mind, I began to feel changes in my body, even though I had arrived in the hospital suffering from malnutrition my breast began to feel heavy, my nipples were tingling. At times I felt nauseous. I had completely lost track of my last period. Suddenly a nagging thought began to sweep through my mind.

I was pregnant. I hadn't had my period in a long time!

My thoughts turned immediately to Father Angelo. That debased priest had planted his seed inside me. At that moment if I could have sent him deeper into hell, I would have.

At first I felt repulsion for this being that was now developing inside me, however minuscule and insignificant as it was at this moment. It would be a constant reminder of Angelo, as if an unwanted reawakening of him was going to appear once again, while his body still decayed deep in the lake.

There would be other implications of course there was Lucius, he'd been out of the picture for what seemed like an eternity. Unless he'd been mortally injured in battle, he'd be back, returning to a pregnant wife, one with a priest's seed inside her.

There was one nurse, Sister Bertina, who unlike most

of the other stony-faced nurses, who I thought might be the only person I confide in, concerning my condition. Of course, she would naturally assume it was my husband who had impregnated me. This was going to be my unflinching version from now on. It would involve empowering all my powers of deception.

When Lucius returned there would have to be a lot of explanations as well the pretence that I was a wife ecstatic at having "his" child. How would he react to this news before his departure? Our relationship had proved fraught. How would this news change things? Theoretically he was going to have something he wanted desperately, an offspring, an heir.

Sister Bertina received the news that I believed I was pregnant with unbridled joy "Mother of mercy, sweet Jesus, a baby what great news she extolled in rapture, adding your husband will be delighted." I offered a forced smile.

"You must eat, nourish that baby of yours, your appetite will grow," she said prudently. I nodded and mumbled a weak "yes" in response to her advice.

"You will have cravings said Sister Bertina with a knowing smile, adding, your body will change, as well as your mind, but the good Lord will look after you."

There could no doctor who could confirm my pregnancy of course, over time the developing foetus would provide the proof. Sister Bertina, naturally, relayed the news to other hospital staff. I should have told her to keep the news to herself, I regretted my oversight. The nurses' attitude to me changed, I was not this woman who had arrived in hospital in highly questionable circumstances, I'd moved on to being a woman to one who was with child. Now when nurses came to visit me, they would talk enthusiastically about the “baby”. This was coupled with the return of Lucius.

CHAPTER 33

Lucius' Return.

He had been informed that I was ensconced in hospital. Despite his weariness he was desperate to see me. My heart raced, while looking out of the window, as I tended to do for long periods of the day until the gloaming light set in, when I spotted him. I had to prepare myself, to be as natural as I could. My mind had been preparing for this moment but still I was ill prepared. There was hardly any time from the moment I first noticed him to his rapid entry.

"Oh Lucrezia he rejoiced, finally a baby, oh I am so happy, my beautiful Lucrezia."

The joy on his face was effervescent. This despite the fact that he was dishevelled and had lacked sleep. He'd returned from some far-off unknown destination.

"Lucius you're back safe," I said trying but failing to equal his joy. He felt like a stranger to me, somebody I hardly knew or was connected to. He rushed towards my bed lent over me and kissed me.

The kiss, in a way repulsed me, but what could I do? I couldn't reject him, or my ruse would fail from the start. I could smell his sweat, he hadn't bathed for a long time, as if he was a hobo who'd been drifting from place to place in the countryside. His beard chafed my smooth skin. The kiss completed, he began to get extremely sentimental, talking about the baby's future.

"Of course, he will have to go military school, we have a long history of soldiers in our family, perhaps he will become a General, imagine Lucrezia, the first general in the Di Benvento family."

He was making a presumption that I was going to bare him a son and I wasn't sure of the idea of bringing a son into the world to potentially die at a later time on the field of battle. I couldn't find it in myself to indulge him with his fantasies. I barely nodded my head.

"Why are you here? Lucius demanded, is it because of the baby, you're not ill, are you?

I answered, "I was ill for a while, but I am better now." Some concern appeared on his face.

"Nothing serious I hope, you have to be in perfect condition to have our baby, I can hardly wait to name him of course he will have to have a Di Bevento name and be christened in the regimental chapel, all the men will have to be present, it will be the prestigious occasion ever, it will go down in regimental history, can you imagine Lucrezia."

However, my mind wasn't imagining any of this, my baby's life was already set out before him, and Lucius' return wasn't what I needed. What I did need was some kind of tranquillity, my soul was still in torment.

Lucius continued for a while with bursts of rapture for this unborn child, then took his leave, I saw him almost cavorting across the pathway from the hospital, in a totally unmilitary manner.

Was I better off in this hospital or was I better off back with him. Why had they kept me so long? Was it more because of my mental state or physical state? They might believe that my mental state was now fixed now my husband had returned. I felt strong enough, after all - hadn't I managed to throttle a priest? Admittedly he was a frail one.

I asked Sister Bertina when it was anticipated I might be released. She laughed. "I suppose you must be desperate to return to that husband of yours, but before this we need the doctor to give you a thorough examination, there's the baby to consider." The doctor arrived soon afterwards, I was weighed and examined and then told in a day I would be fit to go.

The next day Lucius arrived with a beaming smile. He was clean shaven and looked revived after his exertions, and he did not reek of the smell of travel and living rough.

"Lucrezia darling, let's take you home," he rejoiced. Slowly and methodically, I dressed. Courteously I thanked some of the members of the hospital staff and shuffled slowly along the long corridors of the hospital, then down the stairs, out into the strong sunlight. Lucius kept talking to me, but his words were of little interest. I couldn't absorb them, my mind was far removed from him, in truth I was struggling to connect with him.

When he opened the house door, I noticed the room was filled with flowers.

"What do you think?" Lucius said, smiling proudly. It was obvious he had made a big effort to welcome me on my return. The military man had discovered another side to his persona, but all of this was being spurred on by the baby that at this point was probably smaller than the size of pea. It would have a pulse, it was within me, I felt it.

"You need to rest a lot my darling Lucrezia, the doctor told me," Lucius said urgently. He'd moved the furniture around and brought down a small divan which had been liberally covered with cushions. There was a big array of fruit on the table; lemons, figs, grapes, quinces as well as other things he deemed would supplement the baby's growth. He was like a new person. Before this he couldn't remotely be considered an attentive husband. I was to him a bauble, to show off in front of other officers, especially when there was some prestigious ceremonial occasion.

All the other wives were model wives, succumbing to their husband's whims. Of course, everything was provided for me, the married quarters, some servants that cared for the domestic aspect of things. I had lots of time on my own, I read a lot, I went for solitary walks in the woods, when I felt strong enough. I was letting time and my life flitter away. I constantly put myself through lots of self-analysis. Who was I? What was my purpose in this world?

CHAPTER 34

Questioning my Faith.

What of my relationship with God? The anger I had vented towards God, after what had happened with Angelo, I anticipated, would never abate. My faith in God had never been at all strong, despite my parents trying to impose it upon me. I didn't know a single soul who didn't go to church with regularity. If they didn't perform this duty, they would surely be considered outcasts and worse still damned. I just went along with the flow and would never have dared question my parents' fervent beliefs. Even at the convent I was sent to for my education none of the girls would question all they were told and if they did the punishment would surely have precluded any kind of blasphemous words, even if they were felt deep down.

But perhaps in my present state, did I not need God? Could God be my saviour? My only hope when all I could envisage was a forlorn destiny. I tried to focus on what I could demand of God, what kind of relationship I could forge. What could I do? Should I pray? If so for what; forgiveness? I had murdered a messenger of God, but he had violated me, surely his death was merited. God would surely understand, was God not compassionate and didn't his son Jesus take away the sins of the world.

Was I really the sinner or the sinned against? Surely Angelo the priest had a corrupted soul and didn't merit the title of priest, which had been bestowed upon him, at his ordination. He might have given the pretence of being a priest but deep within he was an evildoer, who for the sake of others I had dispatched from this world. Did this make me a soldier of God?

With Lucius coming and going I had time to think about such matters. Pregnancy seemed to be long and laborious, I had moments of deep anxiety and moments when I could hardly believe what was happening, while at the same time I was exhausted and run down, I needed plenty of rest, I had a strange taste in my mouth and my breasts felt more tender than they ever had before. Sometimes I experienced mood swings, one night I screamed at Lucius.

"I don't want to live this life anymore!" Of course, he was mortified.

"How can you say such a thing, you are going to have a baby, for the love of God."

"It is me who is going through all of this, the pain, the anxiety, as this thing grows inside me."

The word "thing" seemed to resonate uneasily in his mind.

"You are talking about my own flesh and blood," he shouted. Of course, I didn't want to contradict him, the consequences of this would be unimaginable.

I relented, "Lucius, I'm so sorry, it's just that my emotions are all over the place at the moment, you understand I hope, the baby will be wonderful and will bring us great joy, I'm already making some clothes for it."

I picked up some clothes from a drawer, I'd hardly spent any time on them if truth be told, I worked on them for half an hour and got quickly bored and uninspired. I'd dumped them in a drawer and had almost forgotten I had started on them. When I produced my paltry efforts, that looked little more than rags, Lucius' face lit up with pure joy.

"These are wonderful, my darling Lucrezia." He almost did a dance and would have looked decidedly ridiculous if he had. I cringed profoundly inside. I suppose in his mind I was turning my attention to the baby; I was but not in the manner he anticipated. How would I relate to it? What if I felt a need to harm it. What if I simply couldn't manage, living with this thing that was going to arrive, that I would be forced to hold in my arms, give it milk from my swollen breasts. It would cry and break my sleep, I would be forced to give it love, that's what would be expected of me.

To appease these intrusions, I indulged in the idea that I would be provided with a nurse to soften the immediate problems after childbirth, then there would be a nursemaid, who would occupy themselves with it, perhaps taking over my role, acting as a surrogate, maybe even indulging it with affection, only sporadic attention on my part would be required. When it would get to the age of entry to military academy school it would be out of sight for long periods. God forbid I was about to give birth to a girl, she would surely hang around for much longer, till she reached the age when she was eligible to marry, she could be sent off to some convent on the other hand.

CHAPTER 35

An Unwanted Visit.

One day I was resting, my body struggling to support this growing foetus, when there was a knock on the door. I felt aggrieved by the fact that I had been disturbed. I shuffled edgily to the door. Lucius was going about his military duties; I was all alone. Slowly I opened the door and found Father Rosario standing with a sizeable grin on his face. My heart sank, what did that young zealot want of me? Whatever, I was not in any kind of state to receive him.

"What wonderful news," he rejoiced as he crossed the threshold unabashed. I could hardly send him away despite feeling I could not stand to spend any time with him.

"Yes, it is," I repeated more out of duty rather than anything else.

He laughed, "and there was me thinking you were ill when in fact you were carrying a little baby, a little gift from God."

If I could have thrown up all over his black cassock and blamed it on the "little baby" I would have done. Instead, I just smiled weakly.

"How are you feeling, hopefully well, blooming with motherhood."

"I have my days," I conceded. "Yes, a pregnancy can be a burden all women share, but I am sure the blessed Mary mother of Jesus will look after you from the heavens above, along with all the heavenly angels."

It seemed like the man had come to give me a sermon. I didn't respond to him. Maybe he felt that now I was pregnant, I was more malleable than our last encounter.

"Sit down, why don't you," I said gesturing towards a sofa. He duly sank down into the sofa and crossed his legs. Thoughts of Father Angelo started to stream into my head, as I remembered our previous conversation. I suppose I simply couldn't resist playing with fire, despite my head telling me that I should be steer well clear of the subject of Angelo to evade any tenuous links. In a voice laced with false concern I said, "Any news of Father Angelo? I suppose he is back with his flock, haven't seen him for a while however." Father Rosario looked vexed, he'd come presumably to talk about the baby, and I had directed the conversation towards a totally different matter. His usual composure was not evident when he responded,

"Father Angelo is still absent." It seemed like he wanted to elaborate, but there was nothing much he could detail. I gave a look of surprise. "Oh, but the last time we spoke I thought you were sure he would quickly rejoin his flock."

His response was weak and unconvincing. "I'm sure wherever he is, God is looking after him." I didn't want to contradict him, certainly not point out that he was in fact decaying, surrounded by algae, entrenched in mud.

"I am sure he is in God's hands, but my mind still wonders where exactly he is?"

The young priest sighed, "Perhaps he's gone to a place of solitude, he's doubtlessly fasting and constantly praying, offering himself to God, he's always been a wonderful servant of God, despite being new to the priesthood."

"Maybe," I responded, "but surely he's absent without the authority of the church, if he's gone astray."

Maybe Signora Di Benvento, your concern for Father

Angelo is most touching, but surely you have other matters to think about, the lovely baby that through God's love is going to arrive in this world." He'd succeeded in shifting the subject, I couldn't goad him anymore concerning Angelo's truancy.

"I have much to think about," I replied curtly.

"Well, I trust you will bring this child up with the word of God," exhorted the fervent priest. "I am sure that somebody like you will ascertain that I do," I replied with a disgruntled voice.

CHAPTER 36

The Fight for the Unborn's Soul Begins in Earnest.

"Signora Di Benvento," said the priest unabashed by my blatant antagonism, "I feel confident in your husband's long absences I will be at hand to give the child religious guidance and you never know perhaps one day they maybe one of God's servants."

I shrugged. "You can't talk Father Rosario about a being that hasn't even been born, it seems you men are all the same, different presumptions, for my husband the child is set for a high-ranking military career." Father Rosario offered a wry smile.

"Of course a military man would think like that, but above all things, every child is a child of God and doubtlessly follows a life of God, if called so to do."

"Father Rosario, did you come here to tell me this?" I added, "have you come to claim the unborn infant's soul already"?

"Signora Di Benvento I have noticed you seem to have a rather unnatural hostility towards me, maybe, you have something that angers you, the last time we spoke, might I suggest if you have something you need to tell God, you confess it to release your burden."

The young priest smiled at me, that horribly smooth voice made me feel nauseous, indeed his whole demeanor repulsed me. If I could have stopped him from speaking, I would have, using any means. My mind was a cauldron swirling with pure hatred.

I had not thought in a long time about confession, I only did it out of compulsion, nothing else. If God is all seeing, watching over us, then where is the need to say in front of a priest the bad things we have done? My life was uneventful. What had I to confess?Well, up to the point, I dispatched Father Angelo. However, I was hardly going to tell this to a priest, I would find myself the most reviled woman in the country and would find myself in the annals of history for damnable reasons. I would be forced to invent minor sins while concealing my more major sin, but what purpose would this serve?

"Father Rosario, since my first moment of meeting you, I have found you lacking in fundamental sensibilities. Not everybody sees the world as you do and yet you seem to have this interminable need to impose yourself on other people."

The young man of God shuddered at my audacity. I doubt anyone had ever called him into question in his faultless life. I observed him as he fought for words. Only propriety probably stopped him from charging out of the house, which would have certainly pleased me.

"Signora Di Benvento, how could you imagine otherwise, my vocation in this life is to spread God's word, and most God-fearing people do best to heed the words of God."

"There you go again Father Rosario, I said, shaking my head scornfully, have you been like this since you were a child?"

"Well yes I found God, when I was still a boy," replied the priest proudly.

"And how did you find God?" I demanded, finding myself intrigued by his past, as well as an unexpected curiosity into the life of the young priest.

"I was sent to monastery school, by my parents, where under the strict guidance of the monks I was taken into the arms of Jesus to be one of his shepherds."

"And what of your siblings, you have brothers and

sisters I suppose?"

"I have a brother," said the young priest awkwardly. His head visibly dropped; his body tensed.

CHAPTER 37

A Revelation.

Judging by his demeanour I suspected that there was something particular about this brother and I intended to find out more.

"Oh really, I said, staring intently into his eyes, tell me about him, are you close?"

"Nazario is my older brother, I am afraid even from a young age, his life, how should I put it, has not been a righteous one."

"Tell me more," I demanded, intrigued by the black sheep of the family.

"Nazario was much older than me, my parents did what they could for him, but they could not thwart his descent into evil, they tried everything."

"Such as?"

I interrupted. The young man of God shook his head.

"Punishments simply didn't work and when they sent him to monastery school, this only made him go further astray."

"Didn't the monks thrash him hard enough, to cast the devil out of him?" I said sardonically, a large smile that I couldn't contain, lighting up my face.

The young priest rued the fact that I had unearthed something about his life, which he obviously, no doubt wished I hadn't.

"The monks did what they could, but Nazario was a troublemaker, his soul tarnished, it was as if he was being driven by the devil himself to go about his work."

"Was he born bad?" I demanded.

"He was born from the love of my dear parents, why

he should choose to hurt them so, I could never imagine."

"What did he do at the monastery school"?

"This I can't tell you," said the young priest firmly.

"You mean you won't tell me," I said while playing with a ring on my finger, anticipating he might not remain as resolute as he hoped he might.

"My parents did not want me to ever know about the wrongdoing in the monastery. However, much to my shame, I found out later. His voice dropped to a whisper, "what he did was most ungodly."

"He obviously did something quite unspeakable; I can see it in your face, where did you find out?"

The young priest stared out of the window and avoided my gaze.

"It was at the monastery when I was a pupil there, if you must know, my brother's time at the monastery unfortunately wasn't forgotten."

"Did you know your brother well?" I demanded.

"Not really, my parents kept us apart, maybe they were protecting me, keeping me away from his wicked ways."

I interjected, "maybe they sent you to the monastery with good reason."

"I suppose I have always tried to atone for my brother's profane ways." The young priest appraised.

"Oh, I see you have always tried to be the apple of your parent's eyes, while your brother is the rotten apple."

"My brother has always caused them much pain, while I have brought them the joy of knowing I am spreading God's word."

"What of your brother now, I suppose he might be married, perhaps he has children. Maybe he has repented his ways, while you will never provide your parents with grandchildren."

The young priest's eyes looked the most disconsolate I'd ever seen in the short time I had known him. There was obviously more to tell. Being a man of God, lying was out of the question. It was him in the confessional talking about a shadow that was cast on his life.

"Nazario's never married," he said in a mournful voice. He has a group of unsuitable men friends. He's still a miscreant, I pray for him daily, but maybe his soul is beyond redemption."

"Your brother's going to hell, while you are going to heaven and what of these men?"

"He has got involved with a bad crowd, men, of the worst kind, men who are debauched sinners," he said in a soft voice, holding his head in his hands.

"Have you tried to counsel your brother, perhaps get him to mend his ways, to see the light of this God you so believe in?"

"I did try once to see him," said Father Rosario, his face cowering at the memory.

"I was at seminary school, at the time. I told my parents I wanted to visit him, they warned against this, in fact they implored me. They'd heard some bad things and hadn't seen him for quite a long time, having had a blazing argument. Reluctantly, they gave me his address. In a way what I was doing was out of character, but I was quite a bit younger than I am today.

I imagined he might have changed; I hardly knew my own brother and perhaps it was a raging curiosity that drew me to discover more about him.

I went by coach to the city where Nazario lived. When I arrived at his house there was no answer at the door. I heard from the next house, and I decided I would inquire if the occupants knew of his whereabouts. I was dressed in my cassock, on my head there was a biretta. I was proud to walk the streets dressed in such a way.

I knocked on the door, it sounded like there was some kind of party going on, there was all kinds of whooping. I felt uncomfortable and out of place.

'What do you want my little cherub, love your outfit by the way,' a voice said while scrutinizing me. I was taken aback by this man's affected voice and blatant lampooning of my clerical clothing.

'I am looking for Nazario,' I said in a hesitant voice.

'You have come to the right place, but Nazario has his hands full at the moment and I don't think he would appreciate being disturbed by even a sweet looking thing like you in a dress.'

'But I am his brother, I exclaimed'.

'Oh dear, little brother has turned up, out of the blue in a dress.'

'It's a cassock actually and I attend seminary school, I am going to serve God,' I said defiantly. The man, who had long hair down to his shoulders, wore a corset and was obviously wearing makeup. I had never seen anyone like him before. In his hand he had a bottle of red wine. He'd obviously consumed a lot of alcohol; he could barely stand up straight.

'I'll just go and see if naughty old Nazario is free to see you, or if he is on the job, if you know what I mean.' I was left standing on the doorstep. I could hear the noise from another equally rowdy party in a nearby street. I imagined the area was teeming with men like the one I had just spoken with, the thought made me feel more uncomfortable.

'Brother' a voice exclaimed, Nazario staggered to the entrance to the house, propped up by the man who had gone to find him. The two of them could barely support each other, it was like two infirm old people trying to remain upright. Nazario's hair had also grown long, and he had obviously not shaven in a while, what was more he seemed to be wearing large earrings and a big medallion round his neck. For a shirt he seemed to be wearing a flimsy women's silk night dress. He looked ridiculous in my eyes, but he seemed to care little about propriety.

'Little Brother, what brings you to this wonderful abode, are you ready to party the night away, the house is flowing with wine and good company, and I see you are dressed for the occasion.'

'I just came to see you in fact Nazario, I didn't expect to find you in such company, our parents still worry about you.'

'Of course, they do, of course they do, they wouldn't be parents if they didn't worry. Come on in little brother, the night is young you should open your eyes to the many pleasures of this fine city.'

I was ushered into a room which was full of mostly men, all in skimpy clothing. There were bottles strewn everywhere. Some of the men were lying on top of each other. Two women in a doorway clutched onto each other. I felt obliged to run out of the house and away from this abomination.

"Why didn't you?" I demanded.

"I should have," replied Father Rosario with a pained voice.

The young man of God complained, Nazario was happy to have his own younger brother corrupted by these depraved sinners. Nazario poured me a glass of red wine, which I needed to calm my nerves. I hardly got to say many words to Nazario. What was there really to say, I had discovered him for what he really was. A man beckoned him over and that was the last I saw of him.

When the man who had opened the door, came over to me, took off my biretta and began to stroke my hair, I ran to door, the man tried to grab me, but I was too quick for him. I ran down the street, a voice shouted, 'you didn't want to go in there, young priest'. I ran and ran to get as far away as I could from this perversion, that I had witnessed.

I suddenly found myself running towards a church, the doors were open, there was evensong going on. I ran through the doors, as if I was running away from a fire. The congregation including the priest stared at me, surely amazed at my bold entrance. I slumped onto a pew and began to pray. Could God cleanse me from what I had witnessed? My own brother was part of this band of deviants, and he'd only wished to parody me, there had been no brotherly connection. He just wanted to crush a beautiful pure image I had of the world by introducing me to his sick world."

"The priest and the pervert" I said to reinforce his pain. There was little he could say to contradict me, he accepted what I said like somebody who has just been given some penance.

"Have you seen your brother since?" I asked, with my curiosity running amok, to see if there was more to this tale of the wayward brother.

"No I haven't" replied Father Rosario, "Neither have I heard any of his news, my parents dare not speak his name, he has brought shame on my family."

"Perhaps he simply chose his own route, while you chose yours."

"He chose the devil's highway, while I chose to follow Jesus' steps," replied the priest indignantly.

At this point Lucius returned.

"Father Rosario, he proclaimed, a strong smile fixed on his face, I hope you have been filling Lucrezia with spiritual words, now she is blessed with child."

Father Rosario winced and found it hard to respond immediately. He was still doubtlessly preoccupied with his errant brother.

"Well yes Capitano Di Benvento, he replied, adding with contrived cordiality, but I mostly came here to check on Signora Di Benvento's well-being at such an important time."

"That's most thoughtful of you Father Rosario," said Lucius smiling warmly at the young priest.

"My wife is a picture of health, wouldn't you agree?" said Lucius, turning to me with delight. After he felt that he had completed his purpose the young priest said.

"Perhaps I should take my leave Signora and Signor Di Benvento."

I smiled weakly at him, I suspected Lucius had noted my lack of enthusiasm for the man of God, but I could not be sure. After the door had closed, Lucius turned to me.

"Nice of him to call round," said Lucius smiling enthusiastically while the priest walked sedately down the path, probably to bother some unfortunate soul.

I simply answered "yes" in an indifferent voice.

I had this disturbing notion in my head that Father Rosario was going to be a permanent fixture in my life, somebody I could not shake off. Each reappearance would rouse equal measures of displeasure. On the other hand, I had discovered something about him that aroused my curiosity, that brother of his. During a rather banal dinner with Lucius my mind veered constantly away to my conversation with Father Rosario and his wayward brother, my mind tried to imagine a more concrete picture of Nazario than the one Father Rosario had given me. I had this bizarre urge to try to meet him. What would this benefit? I tried to dismiss this idea.

CHAPTER 38

Another Visit.

The next day, while as ever Lucius was going about his military affairs, there was a knock on the door. I knew in an instant who it was, and my natural intuition proved right.

It was Father Rosario as I had imagined, almost on cue, but this time he seemed to be less of the outrageously confident young priest and more of a man with insecurities.

"Signora Di Benvento, if I might talk with you for a moment," he said in a hushed voice.

"Certainly, come in," I said reluctantly.

"Perhaps I spoke too much yesterday, concerning my brother, I should have been more circumspect. All of the things I told you I should have simply kept to myself. I feel shame now, I hope you understand Signora Di Benvento."

I smiled at him, a mischievous smile, rather relishing his fragility.

"So, what do you want me to do, erase everything from my memory, pretend this conversation, never happened, for a change you showed you could be honest with somebody, now I suspect you feel vulnerable, am I not right?"

"I can't deny what you are saying, Signora Di Benvento, I was not my usual assured self yesterday, I made a mistake, you do understand Signora Di Benvento? He continued in a hushed voice, now I feel embarrassed it is true and now I implore you in Jesus' name not to repeat the words that were told in confidence and not compromise my standing within the community."

I smiled sweetly at Father Rosario and in my most mellifluous voice I said,

"But Father Rosario, how could you think such things of me that I would wish to sully your good name, by telling people of your brother. Anyway, people should judge you by your actions, not those of your brother."

"Oh, thank you most kindly Signora Di Benvento, I will always remember your discretion and diligence concerning this delicate matter."

Of course, I was just playing with him, the subject was not closed, by any means and I meant to exploit it.

"How many people know about your brother and his wanton lifestyle?"

"None if truth be known, my parents have told everybody that he is travelling the world."

"Surely they are lying to the world," I said sending a sharp pang of pain to the young priest's face.

"You are right Signora Di Benvento of course, but think of it from the perspective of our noble family, what purpose would the truth serve?"

"The truth will always be there, despite your parent's efforts to divert it otherwise," I said, shrugging my shoulders.

"My parents are God loving people, whereas my brother is a..."

"A man who, from your account, seems to prefer the company of men, rather than women."

Father Rosario, looked horrified, my blunt words disturbed him greatly.

He began to be angry with himself. He began to think out loud.

"I knew it, yesterday I made an appalling mistake,

which you lured me into, what an idiot I am."

"How did I lure you? I simply asked whether you have any siblings."

"But then you seemed to beguile me into saying things I would never normally divulge to a living soul." The young priest's face was bitter at the thought.

"Did I contrive some kind of magic?" I asked followed by a little chuckle.

"You are having fun at my expense Signora Di Benvento, I imagined you had a heart, but it appears you want to profit from a most unfortunate situation." I feigned being contrite.

"I am so sorry Father, I didn't mean to cause you any embarrassment, and like I said I will keep the story of your brother fully in my confidence, I can assure you, anyway whatever your brother does, hardly bothers me."

"I thank you Signora Di Benvento," said the priest, who I seemed to have appeased.

"Perhaps after all your anxiety, you might care for a drink of some kind." "That's very kind Signora Di Benvento, but I really should be going, I have the hospital rounds to do."

"Don't let me keep you from your good works Father Rosario."

We exchanged weak smiles and Father Rosario, left the house. I am sure he had grave doubts about me, that somehow, I could inflict harm on him at a later moment. I delighted in the thought. I did not see Father Rosario for a while, instead I was confined to my home, as I wiled away the rest of this interminable pregnancy. The thing inside me began to agitate me more and more. I began to get impatient I wanted this thing which was inside me to be extracted out from within me.

At the same time, I was worried bordering on terrified. I was often moody for no apparent reason with Lucius, this anger swelling up from within, knowing of course he was not the father and culpable for this thing that was implanted in me.

I was also prone to weeping endlessly as I spent lonely hours by myself. I began to hate my body appearance, this vile ever-growing bump. Did the baby within already feel some kind of hatred towards it? Was my brain already sending signals to it, disturbing it before it had already been born? Did it sense it was going to be born into an environment in which it wouldn't be wanted from its maternal side?

CHAPTER 39

Bad Behaviour.

While all of this resonated in my mind, Lucius seemed to get ever euphoric about its impending arrival. He just wouldn't leave the subject alone. When other couples were invited to dinner, these relentless references to this unborn entity reached sickening proportions. My mind was screaming "shut up"! However, he kept persisting with his endless fantasising about the baby's future, as if the child was destined for a life of never-ending glory. Never had such high expectation been placed on an unborn. During one such dinner with another military couple I had to excuse myself, explaining I wasn't feeling well, which was not the truth, it was more my mind that was unwell.

Lucius and the other married couple Antonio and Fiore Romagnolis (who were blissfully married, already blessed with two children) were duly shocked and concerned, but I simply just had to get away. I certainly killed the party, but this gave more pleasure rather than guilt. I heard them talking in hushed voices, no doubt expressing their concern. Lucius came upstairs to find me in darkness lying in foetal position on our marital bed, still fully clothed.

"Are you all right?" he demanded in a concerned voice, the Romagnolis' think it better they leave, on account of the fact that you are unwell," Lucius said in a forlorn voice.

"But surely they have not had their main course or dessert, and Aida, spent a long time preparing a fine meal, I am quite happy being here on my own."

"I suppose you are right Lucrezia, but are you sure everything is all right, the baby is fine I suppose?"

"As far as I can tell Lucius, now you go downstairs and explain that they should not have their dinner ruined by me. Perhaps you might find other things to talk about rather than this baby, that will arrive in due course, I did find the dinner conversation so boring."

I realized what I said had pained Lucius greatly, if Antonio Rogmanolis and his meddlesome wife hadn't been downstairs a massive argument would have broken out, that was for sure. Instead, he tried to compose himself to face once again the couple, who were downstairs, wondering what exactly was going on, and what to do.

"She's a little tired that is all but said we should carry on the dinner in her absence," proclaimed Lucius, in an unassertive way. Fiore expressed her concern again and the conversation continued in a stifled way. The meal didn't finish as was anticipated. No doubt they religiously ate the meal the cook Aida had provided. I heard an exchange of farewells and the stodgy couple asked Lucius to pass on their best wishes to me, which of course he said he would. While dinner was progressing, I slipped out of my clothes into my night attire and waited for Lucius to arrive. I heard him shuffling upstairs.

"Lucrezia, darling, are you alright?" he inquired in a quiet voice.

"Yes Lucius, I am fine, I just didn't really fancy the idea of an evening with the Rogmanolis, talking about babies."

"But surely Lucrezia the baby's arrival heralds such joy and the Rogmanolis', are all too happy to give advice. Antonio Rogmanolis is one of the regiment's finest and Fiore is adored around the barracks, both are delightful company, we are lucky to have them as friends."

"If you say so Lucius," I replied unconvincingly.

"I know it can't be easy in your present state Lucrezia, but please make an effort when we have such company, even if it's just for propriety's sake."

"Lucius I will try my best, but I don't think you can imagine a pregnant woman's feelings and emotions, any more than I can understand a military man in the field of battle."

"I suppose you have a point Lucrezia, there," conceded Lucius, while he took off his clothes and put them folded on a chair. He climbed into bed, and I pretended to fall asleep quickly, to evade his attention, but the reality was that my mind was still very much alert, churning through a multitude of dark thoughts concerning the future that lay ahead.

After my behaviour during the Rogmanolis' visit, Lucius decided to curtail dinner parties at our home and no invitations were forthcoming. It was obvious he was getting more dismayed by my mood and comportment. I was simply too precarious for him and perhaps if I continued in such a way, people in the barracks would begin to talk. Recent events including my stay in the hospital probably had aroused unwanted gossip as it was. There was Lucius' image to maintain, and a capricious wayward wife was totally undesirable within the insular walls of the barracks.

CHAPTER 40

Family Concerns.

My family also seemed to show concern as to my state of mind, my sister demanded "Lucrezia, are you sure you are all right, it's fine between you and Lucius, isn't it?" Little did she know, Lucius wasn't the problem, in truth he was just an irritant, the problem was the foetus that was developing within me spawned by a priest. Of course, I managed to circumnavigate my way past their questioning and contrive an acceptable image of marital happiness.

"Lucius and me, I said with a gentle laugh, of course there is no problem, we are expecting a child, however you could imagine such a thing."

"It just seems that Lucius seems to have concerns about you, he doesn't seem to be his usual flamboyant self."

I rebuffed her sentiments.

"It's all quite normal we are expecting our first child, and his military work is, as you can imagine, arduous."

"I suppose you are right," conceded my sister, still showing anxiety on her face. On another occasion Mother also expressed her concerns, to which again I was forced to be equally deceitful. Mother proved harder to convince. I faced an afternoon of her incessant questioning as well as a fair share of lecturing concerning keeping a husband happy.

Had Lucius been talking about some of my antics? I imagined his rigid military mind would have curtailed him from talking about emotional matters with my family. Doubtlessly he would prefer to conceal my behaviour from the outside world, pretend it wasn't happening, rather than face any kind of undesirable indignity.

My days were now confined to the house, in readiness for when I would be taken to the hospital to deliver this abomination that was growing and now kicking about, causing me terrible back pain, causing me heartburn as well as other discomforts. How I longed for this childbearing episode to be over, but it seemed to me to be interminable.

Lucius was unexpectedly sent away on a mission. Maybe for the first time ever he cursed being given some orders. There was the inevitability that he would be away, while I would be giving birth. In a way this sudden turn in events suited me. Not that he would be present during the actual childbirth, but he would be there in the immediate aftermath, no doubt swooning to everybody about the new arrival.

CHAPTER 41

Giving Birth.

A few days after his departure, in the morning of a hot July day, my contractions grew more intense, and I found myself breaking water. A nurse had been assigned to watch over me and, on her orders, I was transported to the hospital, so that my condition could be vigorously monitored. The nurses tried to offer me as much comfort and reassurance as possible. The next four hours were to prove hell for me. If I hated the being that was about to exit my body before, I hated it even more now, due to the pain that accompanied it. With screams of pain, I finally pushed the creature that had resided in me for nine months out.

The midwife and nurses delighted in the delivery. It was revealed, with much glee, the wretched infant was a boy. I kind of half expected this, a boy would remind me on a daily basis of Angelo, doubtlessly he would inherit his looks.

CHAPTER 42

Cold rejection.

I heard the baby crying, it was alive, its constant howling repulsed me. It's cries were for me no doubt. It was soon wrapped in clothing and presented to me, to my mind, an unwanted offering. Its eyes were firmly shut, but I felt like its eyes were boring in on me. It was demanding and it kept on shrieking.

"Won't it stop?" I said out loud, with a voice of desperation.

"Don't worry you have a healthy baby with a big set of lungs," said the Midwife, trying to heighten my affinity with the newborn.

"Take it away from me!" I demanded; my eyes fixed on the open door.

"But Signora Di Benvento," said the midwife in shock, "you need to bond with your lovely baby. What a beautiful baby boy you have." No superlatives could convince me that what I had in my arms was not causing me to feel warmth or any remote form of love; it was making me feel loathing and despising.

With my obvious rejection, the nurses had to tend to the child without me, one of them holding the still howling creature, tightly in her arms, trying to sooth it. It was cleaned and then clothed.

"Don't you want to hold it?" implored a nurse, who had seemingly fallen in love with infant, hoping I mighty quickly relent, which I didn't.

"I have made myself perfectly clear, I don't want any contact with it. I would prefer you just take it away and leave me alone."

There was a cot the baby was meant to stay with me, we were supposed to slowly begin our lifetime of a strong attachment, as mother and son, but for me this was unthinkable, given the circumstances of the conception and the absent father of the child, I would not be its mother, under no circumstances, it had exited my body, my work was done.

Then after I had begun to be more phlegmatic concerning the situation, it dawned on me that Lucius as well as my family would not question my rejection of the baby, as well as my mental state. I had to quickly make a new appraisal of the situation, as much as it disgusted me to hold the creature in my arms, I had to, whether I liked it or not. I would have to train myself to resemble some kind of loving mother. I would have to fight against my inner feelings.

"Nurse, I want to see the baby," I shouted out.

There was a brief silence. Hopefully the nurse had not been too shocked by my previous behaviour, putting it down to the ardours of giving it birth and a spike in my hormones. Then enthusiastically the nurse replied, content with my sudden change of heart.

"Signora Di Benvento, that is wonderful news, it's sleeping at the moment, but I'll bring it in, and you can hold it in your arms." The thought repulsed me, but I waited none the less for this "thing" to arrive.

The nurse came in with a broad smile, carrying this "object", now clothed, but not crying. She placed it gently in my arms. As soon as contact was made, it began shrieking more intently, as if I had placed needles in its tiny eyes. It seemed it was conscious that I had rejected it, now it was rejecting me. Fully setting eyes on it I felt I could have been holding a version of Angelo, I thought as it seemed to be thrashing about, trying to break free from me, like a drowning dog trying to get out of a rushing river.

"There, there," said the nurse calmly addressing the still irate infant, as she eyed my struggle to placate and connect with the infant.

"Give the little lad your thumb, Signora Di Benvento, that should calm him down, adding you will start to feed the little lamb in a short while."

The thought of this infant clinging and sucking on my breast, disturbed me greatly. While these dark thoughts circulated in my mind, the nurse ushered in another vexing issue. "What will the little darling be called?" The nurse's eyes seemed to bulge, and an evident smile radiated from her lips. It hadn't occurred to me, that the child required a name. I just grasped at any name that entered my head.

"Daniele," I said briskly without emotion, the first name that entered my head. In fact, I had a cousin named Daniele. I had detested him since I was a child, primarily because he'd pushed me into a pit full of brambles once and laughed as I climbed out, my legs and arms bleeding, while tears of indignity and pain ran freely down my face.

He'd claimed it was an accident, but in truth he'd done it to impress his older brother Davide, who was equally sadistic and happy to see my pain. Even now my distaste for Daniele reigned, and despite all my efforts to distance myself from him, he still managed to irk me with his conceited smile which distended blatantly when he brought up the subject of my encounter with the bramble pit as he often did on numerous occasions without any remorse.

The name Daniele seemed appropriate.

"Daniele," repeated the nurse as if she was musing

on its magnitude. With a beaming smile she said "after the great saint Daniele of Padua, no doubt." I nodded my head in agreement, to keep up the pretence; I could hardly contradict her and say in truth it is the name of an odious cousin.

"The great martyr," lauded the nurse, "who was nailed to a table, dragged by a horse to die of shock and blood loss."

"Is that so?" I replied with a shrug but with little enthusiasm besides.

"He is the patron saint of women whose husbands are at war, how appropriate," said the nurse her verve never waning.

I nodded weakly, thinking perhaps I had chosen the wrong name, this woman seems to be a fountain of unbridled knowledge on this particular name and its religious significance. The newly named Daniele found it appropriate to elevate his screaming, which drowned out the possibility of conversation. His piecing screams doubtlessly punctured the normal tranquillity of the hospital and I imagined further afield, I imagined it was now omnipresent in the barracks.

Fortunately, Lucius was away, so unable to take in the infant's cries. However, on his return he would no doubt soon be doting and drooling all over the infant if he was to discover the truth of the child's parentage his mood would doubtlessly turn to anger.

I called out to the nurse, "can you take this child away, I need some rest." The nurse seemed to take her time to come to my aid. After a time, I vaguely heard some muffled voices, adjoining the approaching footsteps. The nurse was not alone. I should have suspected Father Rosario would make a reappearance in my life, once he had got wind of the infant being born.

He entered the room; his smile was as broad as it was contrived. His eyes immediately latched onto the baby who was still shrieking at the top of its voice, its face purple and contorted with disdain.

"What an adorable little lamb of God," purred Father Rosario, as the infant wriggled as if trying to break free from me.

I didn't reply, what was the point? Despite his odious noise, the baby clenched in my arms, seemed to have won over the priest, with little contest in evidence. He approached the infant and gently touched him, on the head as if giving his benediction, and beamed another big smile. The child seemed to be mysteriously becalmed. Did he think his father had arrived? Rosario was indeed an Angelo duplicate, slightly younger but the two men almost blurred into one being.

Rosario hadn't wasted much time welcoming the new-born into the fold.

Of course, he would argue he was simply on his hospital rounds, doing good deeds. I would have happily handed the new-born over to the predatory priest, but I did not want to afford him this satisfaction. Lucius would claim his offspring for the military, while Rosario would wrench his soul for the church.

The young priest continued his eulogy for the infant.

"He's an angel sent by the divine, Signora Di Benvento, sent to lead this world from sin."

"What would he know about sin? I interjected, adding pertinently, he was only born not so many hours ago."

"What indeed," said the young priest musing, "he's pure, as pure as all the angels in heaven, before Lucifer's fall from paradise."

CHAPTER 43

Bating a Priest.

The infant now seemed to have slipped into a deep peaceful sleep, and it could be confined to its cot. Our bonding session had ended. I anticipated that the infant's exit might hopefully coincide with Father Rosario's departure. As ever the young priest was arduous. I handed over the child to the nurse. Father Rosario again drooled over the child as it parted, doing a little wave with his hand, which made him look ridiculous.

"You should have your own child," I said acerbically. Father Rosario recoiled, in horror.

"As you surely know, Signora Di Benvento, priests are beholden to a life of chastity, devotion to God alone."

"But you are also human, no Father?" "Have you never thought about what you will miss out on, if you never father a child?"

The young priest glared at me, then pontificated. "Children are always close to the heart of the church, Signora Di Benvento remember what Jesus said when amongst children, he beckoned the little children come to him, saying the kingdom of heaven belongs to them."

"I suppose you want my child to enter the kingdom of heaven," I said in a sceptical voice.

"I am sure your child will lead a godly life, with the love of Jesus and the guidance of the church," replied the young priest indulging in the prospect.

"What if he grows up to be like your brother?" I asked to add a bit of spice to the conversation.

"This will never come to pass; I will make sure of this myself," snapped the priest. I delighted in the fact that I had opened a sore wound, one that the priest had hoped I would veer away from, but I was annoyed by a part of his response.

"You will make sure?" I questioned. "How can you make sure, you have no autonomy over this child."

"The child will need spiritual guidance, I would suggest, that I would be the perfect person to undertake such guidance, his father will be away often and as you well know Signora Di Benvento, military life is very precarious and with mortal combat can prove fatal."

The young priest was back on old territory, he had made his case before the child was born, that he should be the guardian of the child's soul. "Am I about to become a widow, Father?" I said with false incredulity.

"God has his plan for all of us," said the young priest, ponderously.

"It seems you have pre-empted a plan for not only my husband but also the infant born not so many hours ago."

The priest endeavoured to retract from proclaiming his visions of the future, "I am sure your husband will live a long life, I have it on good authority, he is the most able of officers and with God's love he will become a wonderful father to his son."

With that it seemed like the priest had succeeded in the endeavour he had hoped to gain from our encounter. He ventured towards the door, then offered a pale smile, when he had reached the doorway, he said, "You must be tired from all your all your labours in bringing a child of God into this world?" I didn't respond, I just delighted as his footsteps trailed away, further into the distance.

CHAPTER 44

A Strange Revealing Dream.

That night I had the most vivid dream. It was inevitable that Angelo would be predominant. However, in this dream he was joined by Father Rosario. Both were equally youthful and fresh faced. I was descending a steep hill. The light from the day was ebbing away. What was I doing? Was I on my way to some kind of meeting? At the top of the hill, I could make out a ruin of a church.

Why was I going there? What was my purpose? I noticed there were some torches burning within the ruin. With the light closing in the powerful flames became more defined, stronger and stronger. Why would anyone be outside in these conditions, in a derelict church? As the hill became even steeper, I found myself slipping, trying hard to keep up any kind of momentum. My clothes began to get saturated in mud and moisture. Somehow, I managed to complete my descent. I was panting, fighting for breath. While loath to enter the ruin, I felt obliged, as if I had surrendered to a force far stronger than myself. I moved timorously to the entrance where all would be revealed to me. The torches seemed to emit blinding light. I was simply bedazzled by the light.

Slowly my eyes were able to focus. There were two men, dressed in simple white robes. Both robes were exactly the same. On further investigation, I made out Angelo and Rosario standing either side of an altar. In the middle of the altar, which had candles burning on each of the four corners, was an inanimate object. After a while I realized the object was a baby, but it was perfectly still, despite being barely clothed and lying on the hard stone of the altar.

"We knew you'd come," both men said in monotonous tone in unison.

I didn't respond, it was like I was a voyeur looking in on a scene, which I had no control over.

"We have much to say," said Rosario after a numb excruciating silence.

"And you have much to confess," said Angelo, in a perfunctory voice, which didn't contain any emotion.

"You killed servants of God," said Rosario, his eyes intent. Angelo gently nodded in accord. I stood there motionless.

"You took away my life on this earth," said Angelo mournfully.

"There was a witness," said Father Rosario in a stern voice.

I shuddered. "Father Piero, saw it all and then told me," said Rosario.

"He was walking by the lake, about to settle down for his customary drink, when he saw two figures. Rosario shook his head, and said in a hushed voice, "He saw you do it Signora Di Benvento."

I was surprised, I had always thought the incident had been a private moment, between Angelo and myself. I'd had some apprehensions after the event, that Angelo's demise had been witnessed, but as time passed by these relented. Father Piero, of all people, I thought, but how could he coherently explain to Rosario, all that had happened, the man was a drunk. Why hadn't Rosario accosted me about the heinous act I'd committed? He'd had plenty of opportunities, also surely it was his duty to inform the authorities.

Rosario's features intensified.

"You also murdered Father Piero, you had the perfect opportunity, your room was next to his, you chose your moment and throttled this man of God to death. It was true I had taken away this man's life, but not for the reasons Rosario had laid out. Rosario continued.

"He was not a man of pure heart, he was not a true servant of God, he was not worthy of his vows to God, but he was a priest no less."

I suddenly became aware of another presence, a sound getting closer, a new fearful presence which I knew I would have to face.

I turned around. Behind me was Father Piero, stumbling, fighting to keep his feet. His face was bitter and mournful. He looked at me still panting, his look chilled me. I wanted to run away but my legs couldn't move, I couldn't control my own body. He was quick to join the accusations, but his language was coarser.

"You killed me, you bitch!" he yelled with a bitter voice, jabbing a finger at me. His eyes looking like there were flames burning within them.

"You are nothing but a murderer, who has committed the ultimate sin, and you will pay for your sins! I may be in hell but, in no time at all, so will you, but in the lower greater depths of hell, from which there is no going back. Let me tell you the wine tastes like brine, burning the back of your throat. The churning seas of hell send sparks that scold the heads of those who reside in hell.

The torment of those in hell is never ending, and it was you bitch, who dispatched me. Now it's your turn to suffer." He held a knife, perhaps the very knife I had used to kill Angelo and rushed in my direction. I screamed and cowered, there was little I could do. He was held back by the other two priests, but not physically, but by them holding crucifixes, that seemed to repel him and weaken his resolve.

When they had taken the weapon from his hand, he seemed to blur into obscurity, melt away, like he had never been present in the first place. My ordeal wasn't over. A new menace came to the fore. The young priest pointed at the child that was lain still motionless on altar.

"We are here to claim your child's soul, it belongs to us, it always has." I tried to plead with them.

"He is my child; it was I who bore this infant."

"Yes, but it was born out of sin, and it has to live a life of goodness to redeem itself, can't you see this?"

"What are you planning?" I asked anxiously.

"You must give up your right to this child, never set eyes on it again."

"I won't!"

I yelled, defiantly.

"But you must, it is the godly and only thing to do". I shook my head vehemently. I began to repeat, as if I was chanting, or saying a prayer.

"It is my child..."

"It is my child..."

"You can't take my child..."

"I tell you; it is my child."

While the priests counter acted, chanting in unison, once more, their voices loud, their faces fervent, unmoving, as they eyed the child.

It is a child of God,
A child of God
A child of God.

CHAPTER 45

All Restrained.

Suddenly I woke up with a jolt, while screaming "it is my child". I quickly realized my wrists and legs were tied to the bed. Sweat was pouring out of my body and my heart was pounding, violently in my chest. Standing next to the bed was my husband Lucius who stared at me, a shocked look on his face.

"Calm yourself darling, you are not well but the doctors tell me you can get better, there is treatment available for you." As he spoke, I struggled, trying to release myself, from the leather straps, that held my wrists and legs, seriously restricting my movement.

"My baby where is my baby?" I cried.

Wishing to be able to hold it in my arms, thinking back to the dream, in which it was so vulnerable and exposed.

"My darling you are in no state to look after an infant, the nuns and priests are looking after it, it will be fine, there was no other choice, not with your mental state, you could have harmed the child. I had to take a bold decision, after what the doctors told me."

"I want my baby, I want to see my child," I shrieked, my mouth was dry, my voice hoarse from all that screaming. Some new doctors came into the hospital room. Despite my wrists being secured to the bed, they felt obliged to scrutinize my volatile behaviour.

"Calm yourself Lucrezia!" one said, a young man who looked as though he was barely out of medical school. He had piercing blue eyes, a soothing voice that also seemed to be menacing at the same time.

I heard the shrieks of other patients. It was clear they were being forced to do things, they didn't wish to do, or were simply uttering strange senseless words, that meant something to themselves, but nothing to others. The noise was relentless, I was obviously in a large ward. Another woman shouted, repeating, and repeating, the same mindless phrase.

"I can fly let me fly, why won't you let me fly?" Another agitated woman screeched, from afar, obviously further away, but still very audible.

"Let me go, I am not mad, it's my husband who sent me, he is the one who is mad, not me." She was firmly contradicted and told to calm herself, later I heard her weeping and wailing.

I was surrounded by the insane, everywhere madness seemed to prevail. What about myself, was I mad, as well? Had I just made many things up in my head? I was at the point whereby I couldn't say for sure what was real and what wasn't. What had really happened and what I thought had happened.

One thing was for sure. I had woken up from one nightmare and slipped into another. Everything was out of my control. My dream had revealed something, my love for my child, yes I did love it, I was reconciled with this fact. Lucius, he had returned from his mission and had been informed of my strange behaviour, following the birth of the infant.

CHAPTER 46

A Conspiracy.

I had been moved from a maternity ward to an institution for the insane. He had no doubt willingly signed all the documents, to keep me incarcerated. I could be here for years, for all I knew. I drifted back into an uneasy sleep. When I woke up, I heard two familiar voices, two men who were standing in the corridor, close to where I was being secured.

"As you are now aware the child was not yours, it was born of the loins of another man, the result of an act of wickedness, it pained me to tell you this Lucius, but I had to."

"This much I have comprehended," the voice of my husband said, forlornly.

The other voice without a shadow of a doubt the voice of Father Rosario, continued.

"So now it is better that it is taken under the wings of the church, so it can find God and in time redeem itself, while your wife is kept safely in here and cannot corrupt the innocent child's soul, you do understand this, Lucius?"

"Yes, I quite understand, it's all for the better, Lucius answered in a soft voice, drawing in a deep breath. The treachery of the man. I'd always thought about Lucius, he never really loved me, I'd always thought about Lucius, as being a man who never really loved me, I was just like a precious jewel to him, who he could show off, when he wished, but as a human being I meant not a great deal to him. It seemed my absence from his life was of little consequence, and as for the child, he was probably happy never to see it. The child meant nothing to him, now he had been acquainted with the fact, it wasn't his. It would be the reaction of most men; he was no different.

In time he would find a new woman, ask her to marry him and beg the church to grant a divorce, how could he be saddled with a mad woman, one that slept with another man and had borne his child? If I had hoped for a saviour, it was never going to be Lucius. I soon began to mourn the loss of my baby. Tears streamed down my face; the pain was too much to bear. As I wallowed in misery some soft footsteps approached, stood in the frame of the small room, painted white, with a cross above the bed, to which I was secured stood Father Rosario.

For a short period, he just looked at me, at my suffering. Finally, he spoke.

"We have your child, now that is all that matters, in fact I have just come from visiting him, a most angelic looking creature, his eyes are surely those of Angelo, but his soul belongs to God."

He had a smug look on his face, like somebody who has just been awarded a great honour. I wrestled to break free, it was hopeless. If I could have broken free, I would have killed him, there and then. He turned and walked out of the room that was now essentially my prison. I heard him gently singing a song, the kind you might sing to a baby to sooth it.

But nothing or nobody could sooth me, I was in hell, as Father Piero, said I would.

PART 3

THE DRUID PRIESTESS

CHAPTER 47

The Strange and Wonderful Milucrah.

Here I am, stuck in a desolate wilderness, until the will to capture me ceases. This is but a forlorn hope. My infamous name will doubtlessly be passed down through generations. For I am damned.

I am fearful of being discovered; my cover broken. Should I be found, I shall surely be slain. For I am a priest killer. This was never my intention. It was simply ill fate.

I was in love with a priestess by the name of Milucrah. We had grown up together in a tight-knit tribe. It seemed our destinies were locked together through all eternity.

I took away her life, at a point when it was flourishing. Many believed she could willfully stir up the seas and the winds by using her magic charms. She was a woman who possessed great healing powers, being a savvy herbalist. I had witnessed her healing a severely injured warrior, with wilted comfrey leaves she had compressed and warmed, and applied to his injuries. Within a few weeks, he was ready for battle again. Beyond this, she was a teacher of children, a fine storyteller, a philosopher and an astronomer, adroit in both mathematics and science.

But it was not just these talents that led me to fall in love with her. Indeed, it was her divine beauty. She was a tall, statuesque figure, with blazing red hair that cascaded down beyond her midriff. Her eyes were both beautiful and mesmeric, her voice was soft and equally beguiling. As she grew into womanhood, I became more and more in awe of her.

As children, we had been close playmates, so much so that other clan members said we were like brother and sister. We would often play by the stream where, in summer, we would run around naked. While her mind was being filled with wisdom, perhaps there was a place in her heart that wished to remain a child at liberty.

When I was starting to reach the age whereby, I would be considered a man, my youthful frolics with Milucrah became increasingly frowned upon.

As time went by, Milucrah's beauty became more pronounced. This had not gone unnoticed by some of the elders, who had obviously developed their own intentions for her. Her body grew strong, and, under the guidance of the great warrior Vercingetorix, she quickly acquired fighting skills.

During one of our, by now increasingly rare meetings, and without warning, she started shrieking before throwing me to the ground.

"So, you have learned how to fight?" I said as my heart pounded. I quickly grabbed her left leg and wrestled her to the ground. The wrestling match that ensued lasted until both of us were out of breath with no energy to spare. I suppose she had done this to show she was equal to a man and was ready to fight, if called upon to go to battle.

CHAPTER 48

First Taste of Battle

It wasn't long before both of us experienced our first battle as active participants. We had previously only watched from afar but were now deemed ready to fight. A local tribe had been rustling our cattle and despite some mediation, no compromise had been found. Revenge could have simply involved recapturing the missing cattle, while taking a few more animals, but the elders had decided that the only way forward was to punish the other tribe to resolve old arguments. Preparations for battle were soon underway, working us all into battle frenzy. Richly decorated weapons were sharpened. The elders consulted a druid for omens on how the battle would develop, and sacrifices were made.

When all was in place, we marched to the field where the battle would take place. We had put lime in our hair and were wearing helmets moulded in the shape of ferocious beasts' heads to frighten to the enemy. Milucrah was there, impressive on her horse, looking formidable. I still harboured doubts in my mind. What if she was slain in battle?

The chieftain gave a rousing speech, saying many heads would be severed and that the enemy tribe would be punished for their insolence. Following this speech, a prophet in a trance began to wail, with predictions of impending doom. Our tribe began to beat their swords against their shields, while screaming insults and battle cries to the enemy at the top of our voices. The members of the enemy tribe responded in kind with their own fearsome racket. The druids stood afar, raising their hands aloft to the heavens, fists clenched. They shouted some caustic curses to the enemy, who cowered in response.

Horns were blown, after which about fifteen men and women raced towards the enemy. Among them was Milucrah, totally fearless. She instinctively charged in the direction of the enemy's most feared warrior, a man called Alsandair, who had been involved in numerous battles, having slain many men. She let out a wild, ear-piecing scream that would have unsettled even the most battle-hardened warrior.

Before Alsandair had time to react, Milucrah had inflicted a mighty blow, sending him to the ground, where he was trampled on by horses. Without the battle really beginning, Milucrah had left her mark, and in so doing, turned the tide of the battle in favour of our tribe. She wasn't finished, again letting out her mighty scream; she succeeded in beheading three more warriors, one after the other, with sweeping blows.

Other warriors of our tribe were inspired by her actions and soon other enemy warriors were slain or severely injured. Having had so much damage inflicted on them, the enemy soon conceded defeat. Only one of our tribe was badly injured, a man by the name of Cadr. Indeed, it appeared Cadr was close to death.

As we were the victors, we duly claimed our rewards. We returned home along with twenty slaves, a lot of cattle, some of which we had won back. We took back some more goods, and some land. We also carried Alsandair's severed head as a trophy - it would be displayed at the entrance of the chieftain's hut for all to see.

CHAPTER 49

The Celebration

A large feast as accompanied by a ceremony to thank the Gods was swiftly decided upon. Spirits were high.

Milucrah was left in charge of caring for Cadr. She had cured others before, but this was a real test of her abilities. Perhaps the elders did not hold much hope for Cadr's survival. Maybe they were too immersed in their revelry, after such a sweet victory. Or maybe it was because Milucrah had now acquired a new status after her exploits in battle.

A cow was slaughtered, then seasoned and roasted on a spit in the round house in the centre of the village. Vegetables - onions, turnips, parsnips, and carrots - were boiled in a cauldron. Some mead pilfered from the enemy tribe was liberally poured and consumed in a few great gulps in drinking horns.

As was our tradition, the chieftain received the largest portion of the booty, but we all profited amply from this victory feast. When all the food had been consumed, Milucrah entered the fray. She told the chieftain that Cadr was now sleeping and that she had attended to his wounds.

"Well, it is time to dance," bawled the chieftain, further animated by the fact that Cadr was likely to survive. Horn players began to blow in unison, while lyre players played delightful melodies. The musical intensity was added to by Crotales, beating a rhythm.

It was Milucrah who took the initiative and began to dance. Her dance honoured the oak tree and sun. The men watched, beguiled while the women were in awe, as she took over the round house with her eloquent moves. After the chieftain had praised her dance, others joined in. The celebration went on well into the night.

A few days later, Cadr was seen walking about. He was a spirited man by nature and here he was, back to his usual self. I asked him how such a miraculous recovery could have happened, and he told me it was all thanks to Milucrah, who had used compressed leaves to soothe and ultimately heal his wounds. Milucrah had once again proved her worth to the tribe. In time, I myself would prove my own value.

News had arrived in the village that a little-known tribe had won a great victory against another local tribe and that among their numbers were some great warriors. We were now seen as a new threat. A few other battle victories enhanced this perception. From being a relatively peaceful tribe, we now found ourselves having to protect our assets, but at the same time a hunger developed to attain new ones.

I became active in battle. I had to improve my sword fighting and weapon handling skills. My overall strength had to develop to be able to fight arduous battles. I went through a regimen of hurling weights, running, leaping, swimming, wrestling and horse-riding. I also had to improve my mental strength. I learned how to project my voice into a fearsome, blood-curdling battle cry. I sometimes worked alone, while other times I learned from the skills and knowledge of seasoned warriors.

CHAPTER 50

A Mission to Prove Myself

To prove myself, I was sent off on a night mission to cut off the head of a rival tribe's chieftain. The idea filled me with abject fear. I had proved myself in a cattle raid of another tribe, but this challenge was far more daunting. I happened upon a chance meeting with Milucrah and explained the ordeal I was about to be put through. Much to my surprise, she offered to help.

"Don't worry, Mordred, I will help you through your mission," she said, putting her hand on my shoulder. I wasn't sure in what form her help would come.

I covertly proceeded by day, still wondering how she would come to my aid, given there was no sign of her. I set off by horse and as I entered the enemy tribe's territory, I found a suitable place to hide my horse. I made the rest of the way by foot. Darkness began to fall and in time, I was close to the enemy tribe's settlement.

It seemed like some kind of celebration was taking place. I heard roars of laughter. Hiding behind a bush, I saw it all. Slave women were forced to dance naked around a fire. I soon realized it was the chieftain's celebration for his impending marriage, as toasts were made in his honour and that of his future bride, who was to be his second wife. All the men were in high spirits.

Suddenly, I noticed what looked like an old woman enter the settlement. Nobody seemed concerned. It was as if nobody had even noticed her. She had brought food and sustenance, which somehow, she had managed to carry on her back. Then I heard some men laughing at her - she obviously posed no threat. There was a huge cauldron and she positioned herself close to it.

What was she doing, I wondered. She discreetly took something out of her bag, and quickly poured the contents into the cauldron. One man had caught sight of her and half-heartedly challenged her.

"It's herbs my dear, just herbs," the old woman said, before cackling to herself.

Before long, the old woman had somehow disappeared - almost as quickly as she had arrived. I stayed by my station, amazed. The celebrations seem to go on long into the night. Luckily, it was a dark night, the moon covered by a thick blanket of clouds. I would have to choose my moment. As I moved gingerly away from my cover, I heard a raven's shrill call. I crawled along the ground slowly but surely, wary of being spotted.

The campfires were dying down. I noticed two dogs, huddled up together, in deep repose, seemingly unaware of my intrusion. Much to my surprise, I saw men slumped over, far from keeping guard as they were bound to do. The whole camp seemed to be in a soporific slumber. Still extremely wary, I made my way stealthily to where I had seen the chieftain go to sleep for the night.

Still crawling, I entered his hut. In the dim light, I saw the chief naked, surrounded by four naked slaves - the ones that had danced round the fire for his entertainment. One of the naked dancers had her arm draped over the chieftain's torso. As I got closer to the chieftain, nobody seemed to move.

One of the girls let out a gentle sigh, as if deep in sleep. I had my sword at the ready. With one abrupt movement, I did as I had been challenged to do. I cut off his head. The blood that spurted out of the Carvilius' head seemed to alert the girls. I expected them to scream in fear, but no words were forthcoming. I quickly understood why. Each of them had had their tongues cut out.

However, I could see the fear in their eyes at the gruesome sight of the decapitated chieftain. I put the head in the sack I had brought with me, should I succeed in my unlikely quest.

CHAPTER 51

Fortune Favours Me

As I left Carvilius' hut in haste, I saw the four naked girls embrace each other, relieved that their ordeal was over. I quickly tried to make my way back to where I had entered the village. A man seemed to stir and in no time managed to jostle his comrade into life. Both sprung to their feet. The ground was slippery, and I feared I might fall over at any moment. I made it to the periphery of the settlement, but I was still being chased by the two men who were trying to stir others to join chase.

I was now in the woods and hoped I could get to my horse, which would give me a great advantage over the two men. A hawk was hovering around above me, as if trailing me, watching over me, as I swerved around trees and ducked between branches.

One of the men was abruptly stopped, a branch catapulting into his face. It must have been providence. I heard him scream in agony as it smashed into him with great velocity. I quickly turned round to assess the situation. He had stopped in his tracks and was clutching his face, which was bleeding profusely. I could not believe my luck, and I kept on going. The taller of the two men was gaining ground, as if energised by his companion's misfortune.

With only one individual left to fight off, I stood a better chance, depending on my combat skills compared to his. I had to calculate when it was best to go on the offensive, and that moment was getting ever closer as my energy was sapped from the running and dodging.

I estimated that if I swivelled suddenly, he might not

be able to stop his momentum and would run straight into my blade. Unfortunately, my plan failed. With the speed of his running, he simply barged into me, before I could lunge the blade at him. I was knocked off my feet but held on tightly to my knife. The force of it caused me great pain, and I wondered if he had not succeeded in breaking my shoulder. It was going to be painful to mount some kind of attack on him. He was a heavy man and he quickly pinioned me to the ground.

I was desperate now. I feared for my life. Suddenly, I heard the sound of heavy breathing. Some kind of animal was approaching at speed, perhaps a wolf? The animal ferociously leapt forward, its claws digging into the man's back. I heard my assailant yelp in pain. He let go of me to fight off the beast. I managed to get hold of my knife and succeeded in jabbing it into the man's chest. Faced with two adversaries, the man was helpless.

The beast tore at his arm, snarling and snapping at him. I managed to manoeuvre the man away from me. The man was now in no condition to fight or defend himself. When he seemed to have stopped moving, I anticipated that the beast would proceed to attack me, but it seemed strangely calm, as if it had completed its mission.

On closer inspection, it wasn't a wolf but a stray dog, panting from exertion. Now it wasn't in combat, it seemed quite an amiable creature, similar to the domesticated dogs we kept in our village.

I started walking slowly, dog following me. This made me feel more at ease with the situation I found myself in. Perhaps there could still be predators hunting me down. I still wondered how I would manage my horse with my injured shoulder. Suddenly, I saw a figure ahead. The dog, however, seemed to have disappeared into thin air, so I would not have its aid this time. I clasped my knife in my operational arm.

"Who are you?" I shouted at the figure, obscured in the darkness of the woods. The shadowy figure didn't answer me. I continued to approach gingerly.

To my amazement, the person who stood before me was the old hag I had seen in the enemy's settlement. I lowered the weapon I was brandishing. She smiled at me. I shuddered – the old woman was unnerving.

"Don't be afraid," she said, smiling again. I winced with pain. She registered my pang of pain and moved closer towards me. Suddenly, she put her hand gently on my injured shoulder. Almost instantaneously, the pain in my shoulder miraculously disappeared.

"Thank you," I said.

"Think nothing of it, go forth and be a great warrior young man," said the old hag before shuffling away to some unknown destination.

CHAPTER 52

Another Cause for Celebration

I was later able to mount my horse and ride off back to my tribe with my trophy as proof of warrior skills. I arrived while people were beginning their daily tasks. A horn was blown to announce my safe return. Members of the tribe were bidden to the round house. The chieftain was to address the tribe. The room listened in silence as he began his speech.

"Dear tribe members, we sent Mordred on a mission, which without the Gods' help we felt sure he was bound to fail. Not that Mordred is not already a great warrior. What he was commanded to do was a tall order. To enter enemy territory and bring back the head of its chieftain Carvilius."

As he uttered these words, he pulled out the head of my victim, yanking it ferociously by the long thick clump of red hair. This act was greeted with a hearty roar of approval. He nodded to his audience in accord, a huge grin mapped out on his face as the cheering became ever more frenzied, before proceeding.

"We expected that Mordred might reach the enemy's gates, but that, faced with the enormity of his task ahead, he would turn back. Our judgment on this young warrior was wrong and now, as you can all see, Mordred is a great warrior who will doubtlessly become a leader of this tribe in years to come. I feel duty-bound to decree that a large feast be held in his honour tonight."

There was another roar of approval, before the abruptly called meeting came to a halt. I spent the day recovering. I marvelled at what had come to pass.

Fortune had looked upon me.

I sought out Milucrah to try to shed some light on these most extraordinary happenings. I found her in her hut, attending to a sick child. She told me she wouldn't be detained for much longer. Once finished, she smiled at me.

"Mordred, the hero of the hour, destined for great things, what do require from me?"

I paused for a moment before replying. "I feel that some mystical happenings occurred during my venture."

"How so?" she demanded.

"I am most fortunate to have survived and I was aided by an old hag," I answered.

She laughed at this. "A great warrior, a rising star, such as you, helped by an old hag?" She began to laugh once more, and I felt quite aggrieved at her flippancy.

"I expected I would fail in my mission, but I found myself inexplicably bolstered, when I got close to enemy territory. I never imagined I would be able to enter Carvilius's hut."

"It seems that the Gods wished that you succeeded. I investigated the omens, and I was able to foretell your safe return."

I shook my head. "It is down to you, Milucrah, that I had a safe passage," I said insistently. Again, she seemed dismissive.

"How on earth could I have helped you, dear Mordred. I am limited in my powers, only the Gods have powers such as the happenings you allude to."

I tried to further illustrate my point. I spoke of the lack of protection afforded to Carvilius, how my two pursuers had come to their ends, including the dog that had appeared out of nowhere and saved my life. And finally, the reappearance of the old hag, who had instantly made my injury disappear.

"I think you are exaggerating my dear Mordred. You should be prouder of your bravery, rather than let imagination get the better of you."

Unconvinced, I left her hut.

The celebration was as raucous as I had expected. I was not really in the mood to celebrate when I felt like I hadn't truly deserved such adoration. The highlight of the celebration was a song sung by Milucrah. The words were familiar to me. It told of a man attacked by a bear, but then a dog came to his rescue and fought off the bear. She smiled sweetly at me as she ended the song.

Applause and cheers broke out. She then proceeded to do a dance. It seemed like she was re-enacting the story she had just told with her song. I, like many others, was enchanted by what we were watching and hearing. When she finished her dance, all joined in a giddy celebration.

I went to sleep that night thinking of Milucrah, her vision and dance movements swirling in my head until I dozed off. The hysteria following my successful adventure was to give way to the need to address its consequences. For the finger of suspicion quickly fell on our tribe.

CHAPTER 53

Bitter Hatred

Carvilius was known to be a bitter enemy of our chieftain Olc. Indeed, they shared the same father but were born of different mothers. They were of a similar age. Carvilius was his father's favoured child. Olc, our chieftain, was bitter and resentful about it. The two mothers hated each other equally and cursed one another whenever their paths crossed. Carvilius's father taught him to hunt, kill wild animals and fish for salmon. Olc was a quiet, reserved child at the time. An opportunity, arose for Carvilius to have some sadistic fun at Olc's expense, when his father took him to visit Olc's mother Brea, who lived with another clan. Carvilius's father had just given him a hunting knife, acquired from a great craftsman who had fashioned an intricate decoration on its blade. Carvilius had not had the opportunity to use the knife yet.

Carvilius had often seen Olc tending to the goats. He obviously treasured these animals. When nobody was looking and feeling his absence would not be missed, Carvilius sneaked to the pen where the goats were kept. One by one, he slit their throats with sadistic relish. The goats had squealed and caused a commotion, and Olc had been alerted. Olc ran towards him.

Snarling Carvilius said, "come nearer and I'll do the same to you." Olc came to an abrupt halt, his anger turned to tears and profuse weeping.

Olc's father approached him. He began to scold him for crying, while not saying a word against Carvilius, who was basking in glory despite his terrible act. Olc's father made light of the matter, adding jokingly, "Carvilius, I gave you this knife to kill wild animals in the forest, not some stupid goats held in captivity, but I suppose you have done the butcher's job, we need to be off now."

Olc's mother comforted him - she knew how much the goats meant to him.

This was not the end of the feud. Another incident occurred when Carvilius arrived with not only his father, but also with a vicious dog. Carvilius was responsible for the brute, holding him by a rope. The dog was generally tied up or secured by a rope - it was well documented that the dog could do untold damage to both man and beast. The hound had even been taken into battle and had all but ripped off an enemy's arm. He was feared and had gained a formidable reputation. Carvilius had spotted Olc innocently playing with his favourite dog, Onora. Without due thought, he casually let go of the rope, setting his brute of a dog free.

The dog sprinted towards Onora and, jumping on him, proceeded to maul him viciously. The sound of Onora's yelps of pain were excruciating, not only for Olc but for other tribe members, even hardened warriors. A man took the initiative. Grabbing a burning branch from a nearby fire, he managed to fight off the brute, whose mouth was now dripping with blood. Carvilius's father then grabbed the rope of the dog.

"Really, Carvilius, you should pay more attention," he said, mildly scolding him while retaining a sadistic smile.

Olc's dog never recovered. The next morning, Olc and his mother dug a shallow pit and, tearfully, Olc buried his favoured dog, while his resentment for Carvilius grew stronger. This incident was not the final one.

Olc now had a half-sister named Tegan. He adored her and felt very protective of her. Carvilius, despite showing no interest in the young girl, noted Olc's attachment to her.

One day, he spotted Tegan all alone. He told his father he was going for a short walk in the woods because he wanted to see if there was any sign of wild boars. His father thought nothing of it. He watched Carvilius trudge off towards where Tegan was playing. His father had some business talking to the elders, he was not in good spirits. He was a little surprised to see his son talking to Tegan, but by now he was more preoccupied with his own business.

Carvilius persuaded Tegan to go into the woods. He told her he knew where they might find some purple orchids, she could give to her mother to make her very happy. The young girl followed him dutifully deep into the wood, paying no attention to where he was taking her.

Hardly a word was spoken between the two. Suddenly, Tegan began to panic. She hardly knew Carvilius and was beginning to regret having afforded him such confidence.

"Where is the place with the purple orchids?" she asked sweetly. He snarled at her. "There is no such place, and now you will do as you are told."

She shuddered in fear. She wanted to get away from this menacing boy, but she had no idea how to get back to her mother's hut. She began to cry, her arms clasped tightly to her chest. She was shivering, partly due to her fear and partly because of the bitterly cold wind - she was dressed in a flimsy gown.

Carvilius demanded that she took off the dress. She

was bemused by his request but obeyed him. He grabbed her tunic and threw it into the nearby stream. He then grabbed a birch branch and began to beat her with it. Her screams were useless and only encouraged him to hit her harder. When his sadistic side was at last satisfied, he calmly abandoned her and walked back to the village. His father had not even demanded that he explain his long absence. When Tegan's mother could not find her sweet daughter anywhere, she became alarmed. The whole village was searched. The whole tribe joined in the hunt for the little girl.

When it was time for Carvilius and his father to return to the clan, Carvilius was seen with an inexplicable smug look on his face. Darkness set in and there was still no sign of the missing girl. The next day, a man was seen carrying a young naked girl in his arms. He had been in the woods searching for mushrooms, when he had chanced upon a slight figure, partly covered by leaves.

Tegan was barely alive; indeed, she was clinging on for dear life. The druid was summoned, and great efforts were made to warm her up and resuscitate her. She had always been considered a delicate child, so her chances of survival seemed limited. Intriguing too were the many wounds she was covered with. People presumed the injuries were not from running in the woods, trying to find a way back home, but that they had been inflicted on her.

It seemed the poor girl had been victim of a terrible ordeal. Olc and his mother had spent the night in vigil. It was clear that the young girl's life was ebbing away. Her breathing seemed weaker. She drifted off into a deep sleep. Then her sleep became more restless. It seemed she was re-enacting what had happened in the woods.

She was muttering words, something that she hadn't done since having been found.

Olc and his mother easily made out the name Carvilius. Why was she saying his name, Olc and his mother wondered. Later, Olc's mother would demand if people had seen Carvilius. Had he been absent for a while? One man said he vaguely remembered him wandering off to the woods, a small child following behind him.

Sweet Tegan slipped away to the other world. Olc's mother seemed calm and serene, so Olc demanded, "Will she be back?"

"Indeed, she will," replied Olc's mother with great assurance, adding that she would come back as a powerful woman, much stronger than before.

Such words didn't stop Olc from mourning his much-loved sister. Sadness then turned to anger. When word spread throughout the tribe that the child had been tortured and left in the woods to die, others began to feel anger. The culprit had to be Carvilius. Most others were accounted for, they had been present at a large council. Normally, Carvilius would always be alongside his father - the two were inseparable. Many knew Carvilius had a sadistic side to him, and some parents had told their children to keep away from him. Both Carvilius and his father's visits to the village were not considered to be pleasurable - more of an awkward inconvenience.

When the father and son visited a week after the young girl's burial, the atmosphere was hostile. Both father and son seemed to behave so arrogantly, with no sorrow at the child's death. When Carvilius's father went to visit Orc's mother, a huge argument broke out, with many accusations and counter-accusations. Fearing for the safety of Orc's mother, the elders thought it prudent to send five of their strongest warriors to take Carvilius's father out of the settlement, along with his abhorrent son. Such an act inflamed tempers even more, and both father and son were indignant about being threatened in such a way. They walked out of the settlement of their own accord, but the bad blood between the clans was to continue long after this tragic episode.

This was not the only tragic episode to befall Orc's mother. Indeed, there were the awful happenings surrounding Tegan's father's death, Owin, some eight years before. Orc's mother, Brea, had fallen in love with a warrior who happened to be best friends with Fiacre, Carvilius and Orc's father. Where there once had been camaraderie (they had gone side by side often into battle) there was only hatred now.

When he heard that Brea was going to have Owin's baby, Fiacre went into a wild frenzy. Although Fiacre had fathered children with different women and had never shown the remotest loyalty to any of them, he couldn't bear the thought of another man being the father of Brea's child. Of course, there was no way of hiding the truth. Fiacre regularly visited Brea and always expected her to be true to him. Owin was a warrior but was also a man who possessed great charm, something which was absent from Fiacre's austere character.

Fiacre was an unpredictable man - nobody could guess what he would do, whether he would enact some terrible revenge. A heavily pregnant Brea went to visit the druid to talk about her condition and find out if the druid could foretell the child's destiny. When she returned to her abode, she made a terrible discovery. Attached to the entrance of her hut was Owin's head. She screamed; many people came out of their huts to see what was going on. Brea continued to wail and scream in shock and horror. The druid led her away from the ghastly sight, trying to comfort her, but she was frantic with grief, moving and shaking violently. For days, she remained by herself, refusing to eat or speak to anybody. The druid begged her to get some food for the sake of the baby.

Then one day, inexplicably her behaviour totally changed, as if her torment had been lifted. Many thought it was due to an intervention of the druid. Perhaps she had seen into the future. When Fiacre came to visit her and "pay his respects" to his great friend Owin, she treated him with coldness and indifference, as she was to do henceforth. This surprised many, who believed Fiacre was the perpetrator of this heinous crime. Who else would go to the trouble of sneaking into the settlement and decapitate a man in a ritualistic form of revenge.

Nobody would dare challenge Fiacre and it seemed such an implausible crime without any clear evidence to pin it to Fiacre. Nobody had seen him that night - it was only the fact that he had such a strong motive that made him a suspect. Lodged in Brea's mind, however, was the belief that Fiacre was unequivocally responsible - perhaps his visits were just made to taunt her.

As years went by, Olc's hatred for Carvilius grew and his spirit became more belligerent. Whenever he encountered Carvilius, pangs of hatred were immediately resurrected. The problem was that opportunity for revenge never arose. Both grew into great warriors and chieftains of opposing tribes. Carvilius was the chief of one of the most powerful tribes in the region. Olc dared to attack his tribe because the retribution of his smaller tribe would have meant they could be obliterated. For all his anger, Olc was a chieftain who cared for the well-being of his fellow tribesmen. In battle he was devastating, but back in the village he was kind and merciful as any chieftain at that time could be. Carvilius on the other hand was a tyrant who ruled by fear and his tribe lived under the continual menace of his cruelty.

Brea, Olc's mother, grew old and sickly. Olc realized her time to pass to the other world was coming. One day, he was summoned to see her. She was confined to her bed and the druid said she had but a few hours possibly to live. Olc remained by her side. She was weak, but she had important things to say.

"Olc, I have had much sadness in my life, but you my son have brought me much joy."

"Yes mother," replied Olc softly.

"Your father did me much wrong," she continued, "but one day a terrible thing will befall his clan and the day of reckoning will come for Carvilius, in the form of a young warrior who will bring about revenge."

She fought for breath but was able to sustain her conversation with her son.

CHAPTER 54

A Strange Occurrence

"This tribe has a great future," she continued, "and you too, Olc, will prove to be a wise and noble leader."

It seemed strange to Olc that a dying woman could have such insights into the future. Olc was to contemplate much of his later life in light of what his mother had said that day, and many years after her death - Olc had become leader of the tribe by then - something strange had occurred.

It was a typical summer day. Everybody in the tribe was going about their business. Suddenly, some of the men and women dropped their tools and quickly made their way in the direction of the woods.

Olc wondered what was going on. Tarlock the woodsman was heading towards the round house, carrying an infant - a little girl - in his arms. Tarlock explained to Olc he had discovered the infant all alone in the woods. There was no sign of any parents or indeed anyone caring for the child. Olc was bemused. He surmised her parents would soon present themselves - perhaps the little girl had somehow strayed. He said that the child should be cared for, and that the druid would be responsible for her.

That night, as he found himself unable to fall asleep, the image of the infant entered Olc's head, and he couldn't get her face out of his mind. There was something familiar about the young girl's face which intrigued him. As he was mulling this over, the image of another young girl resurfaced - a girl from his past, his half-sister, Tegan. He had never forgotten her and what had happened to her. This lost little girl was the spitting image of Tegan. Had Tegan returned? His mother had always said she would.

The next day, Olc went to see the druid, firstly to see the child to confirm last night's thoughts, and secondly because he wanted to discuss his theory with the druid. The young girl was lively and animated, and seemed happy to see Olc, although she could not yet speak properly. His thoughts about the girl had not been unfounded, and he felt a connection with her. This, the druid immediately noticed.

"Have you met this girl before?" he queried.

"I don't think so, and yet she seems very familiar to me," Olc answered, rubbing his brow pensively.

"Oh…" said the druid, aware that Olc was looking decidedly preoccupied.

"In truth, the child resembles my half-sister. I'm sure you remember she too, spent the night in that very wood and died."

"Of course I do remember," said the druid in a solemn voice. After a pause, the druid continued, "I see what you mean. My memories of your half-sister, are a bit hazy, but this child bears an uncanny resemblance to her."

"How can this be, dear druid?" demanded Olc, still awe-struck.

"As you surely know, the dead do come back," said the druid.

"My mother foretold Tegan would return," said Olc.

"I will be happy to help guide the child, Olc, unless she is reclaimed by her parents of course," said the druid earnestly.

"Of course, dear druid, you are the best person to enlighten and guide her."

Nobody came to claim the girl over the next few weeks, and she was given the name Milucrah. And it was I, Mordred, who was to be her companion and playmate.

A few days after my heroic adventure, I was summoned to Olc's hut. This was when he told the incredible things that had happened in his life, in particular about the cruelty of Carvilius and their common father. I listened in awe, marvelling. At times, he interrupted his narration to discuss some point of tribal law, his brain getting muddled - he was getting old.

I had often wondered why Milucrah had been brought up by the old druid, where her parents were, or if they were even alive still. I left Olc's hut full of questions. If Cervilius had been as cruel as Olc had told me, then I had rid the area of a terrible man. Knowing what I knew now of Milucrah made me feel even more rattled by her. The power she possessed set her apart. But then Olc had predicted great things for me. I was to lead the tribe after him and lead our people to prosperity.

CHAPTER 55

Tribes Unite Against Us

News of Carvilius' demise sent shockwaves throughout the area. Although Carvilius had ruled by force and had succeeded in alienating many leaders from neighbouring tribes, the feeling following his murder was one of anger. He would not be missed - indeed, many rejoiced at his demise - but his death was an affront to the natural order of things. His tribe, the Martoks, decided it was a matter of honour to seek revenge, and they joined forces with the mighty Movantae tribe.

The Movantae boasted some of the finest trained warriors, renowned for their horsemanship and brutal methods to vanquish their enemies. They were equally infamous for their horrific treatment of prisoners. They struck fear wherever they went. The Damnolia tribe had also agreed to send five of their fiercest warriors. There were rumours that mercenaries were also coming from far afield to join the fight. A delegation was sent to my tribe, informing us that as a result of our action, revenge was necessary to restore order in the region.

CHAPTER 56

Fortune Again Favours Our Tribe

There was no possibility for mediation. And so it was set in stone, a battle would be taking place, which we had to prepare for. The battle was to take place the night following the fifth moon. The day of the battle was greeted by a thick mist. Rising early, we dressed in our battle wear. We had dyed our hair with lime and painted our torsos with blue insignia. Weapons were sharpened, and rousing speeches and songs were sung to elevate our spirits for battle.

The old druid chanted the sacred incantations before we rode off, still shouting out our resolve that we would honour to the Gods in battle. Heading towards the designated battlefield, the thought occurred to me that I hadn't seen Milucrah around.

She had played a crucial part in the last battle, almost single-handedly swinging the battle our way. She had always been unpredictable, at times leaving the tribal settlement for days on end without any explanation. Her absences had become a common occurrence and no one would have questioned her. She was free to go as she pleased. Regardless, she was a valuable, irreplaceable even, member of the tribe.

I asked Tanguy and Nyle, who were riding beside me, if they had seen Milucrah, but neither of them could recall when they had last seen her, although they were sure she wasn't among us. This was not a good omen.

The enemy was already in position when we reached the battlefield, holding their shields and banners. They jeered as we moved into formation. We started howling and shrieking back at them, then smashed our swords onto our shields, as was customary. Pockets of mist seemed to cover some of the battlefield, from which an unlikely figure appeared out of nowhere – the old hag who had come to my rescue during my mission.

She was bent over, picking mushrooms between the two armies, oblivious to the fact that a battle was about to take place. Holding her wicker basket, she started hobbling closer to the enemy side, who finally noticed her and started laughing and mocking her.

"Old hag, you are about to be crushed to death. Our horses will pulverise you," one man shouted.

Somebody, doubtlessly a mercenary, made some kind of joke in his native tongue, which was met with hysterical laughter. The old hag then joined in the merriment, performing a whimsical dance mocking, it seemed, the enemy troops. They laughed at her, while we stood firm and focused, not allowing the absurd spectacle to distract us.

At the end of her ridiculous dance, she started cackling uncontrollably. The mirth on display started to aggravate the enemy commanders. They had come to obliterate our army, not mock some hapless old hag. If they were not careful, the whole situation could turn into a complete farce.

Regardless of the hag, horns were blown, and fifteen standard bearers started to charge towards us, whilst fifteen of us rode at speed to oppose them. Suddenly, the hag unleashed from her basket a thick, black swarm of flies, which flew into the faces of the enemy, as the hag herself disappeared.

The horses, also disorientated and out of control, could no longer hold the warriors, although some managed to stay on. I picked my adversary, whose eyes were covered in a swarm of flies and choking from the flies that had entered his mouth.

With one deadly blow, I hit his neck with my sword, and his head flew up in the air, splattering crimson blood all over me whilst a riotous cheer greeted me. I didn't care. My mind was now truly in the battle, and I looked and acted the part.

And soon the ground was covered in blood and bodies.

A thick mist suddenly engulfed what was left of the enemy lines still waiting for their turn to join the battle, and when it receded, many a soldier had deserted - likely the farmers and those less expert in the art of battle. Some of the mercenaries had also left the battlefield, knowing already they wouldn't be getting the rewards they'd been promised.

Our warriors were now on the crest of a wave, basking in glory. Yet the battle was still far from over.

Suddenly I found myself surrounded by three Damnolia warriors. There was nobody around to help, and there was no way I could hold off three powerful warriors by myself.

Then suddenly a hawk swooped down and sunk its talons into one of the warriors' faces, blinding him and ripping into his face. The shock of the situation gave me the advantage, and I managed to land a blow on one of the other warriors, incapacitating him so I could concentrate on the remaining one, who proved easy to defeat.

The warrior who had been attacked by the hawk was severely incapacitated, and so with a swift jab, I stabbed him in the heart. The hawk was still hovering around above us, observing what was happening whilst watching over me. I rejoined the battle, which we seemed to be in control of, although we had suffered important losses.

Still, the enemy was not yet defeated, and we needed something to push us towards victory. It could still turn in their favour... Then suddenly I heard some growling and snarling. Coming out of nowhere was the very same dog who had rescued me during my mission, leaping up at an enemy horseman and causing the horse to panic and throw its rider to the ground. Other enemy horses started to panic and throw their riders to the ground. The enemy battle formation was thrown into disarray, as more riders tried hard to control their horses.

The dog vanished as quickly as it had appeared to cause havoc within enemy, who by now only had one option: to fight on foot. As the disorderly rabble of what was left of their army ran towards us, a figure on horseback was racing at speed to join the fight. Milucrah, brandishing a long staff adorned with a skull.

With both arms she swung the staff at an enemy warrior. The blow struck him on the skull, and he crashed to the ground. The next warrior fared no better. Milucrah's horse seemed to direct itself in the direction of enemy combatants, allowing Milucrah to use the staff as a formidable weapon.

One after another, Milucrah cracked the skulls of the enemy or knocked them off their feet. She was quick and decisive and had the advantage of taking the enemy by surprise. Her actions seemed to spur on others in our tribe into action and inflict damage on an enemy that was now facing defeat. A rousing cheer broke out, horns were blown, and our standard raised, as victory was proclaimed.

Milucrah turned her attention to the wounded. Some

prisoners were rounded up. Discussions were started about the rewards of the victory. We had never won such a great battle, for in the past, we had been a mostly peaceful tribe of farmers happy with their lot who had remained at peace with other tribes. Now we had changed our destiny. Power and fortune were now ours to grab.

CHAPTER 57

The Rewards of War

Singing songs of victory and praise to the gods, we headed back to our settlement, taking back with us slaves, cattle, and treasures. We now had more land than we had ever possessed before.

We were greeted by cheers of adulation. Although there was sorrow for those who had been lost, we knew that Milucrah's healing powers would heal many of the wounded. We gathered in the round house to listen to Olc's speech. Horns were filled with ale and passed around – the mood was most decidedly cheerful.

"What a great victory!" Orc bawled, pumping his fist in the air. "The greatest ever in our tribe's history. We have defeated our greatest enemy and we have honoured the gods. I am proud of all of you, and I have heard about some great exploits from some among you. Mordred, you showed once again that you are a great warrior and the future leader of this tribe." To rapturous cheer, Orc held up the head of the warrior I had killed at the start of the battle.

"Milucrah, you've slain many men and killed off the enemy's resistance."

The crowd cheered an absent Milucrah. The roll of honour continued. Musicians began to play rousing tunes and songs were sung before the customary dancing.

As light began to rise, so did Milucrah, effervescent and ready to dance. We were starting to wane, but still looked on in awe. When the dance had come to its conclusion, Olc bade her sing a song to commemorate the battle. The song she sang told of an old woman bravely defying an army.

The celebrations went on for three long days and nights before the tribe slowly got back to its routine. But things had changed, and some already wanted more wealth and prestige to strengthen the tribe's standing in the region through battle victories.

From being peaceful farmers, the tribe had transformed into something else which almost frightened Olc.

CHAPTER 58

Reaching Out Further Afield

After two more great victories, the appetite for conquest spread further afield, to foreign lands. It was I, Mordred, who was charged with leading the raids. Our sequence of victories continued, but I had discovered a new way of gathering wealth that didn't involve bloodshed: trading with foreign powers.

We traded furs, amber, jewellery, weapons, and salt, for which we would get, among other things, wine, pottery, and gold. But it wasn't just objects we brought back from foreign land. We learnt other ways of living, discovered different beliefs, some that involved an almighty discovered in far off lands.

The priests who believed in this God spoke very differently to our druids, about a messiah with special healing powers who had been nailed to a cross before joining his father in heaven.

My standing in the tribe was increasing with each new raid. However, my bond with Milucrah was dwindling because of my prolonged absence. The times we had played in the woods, cut out from the world, were but a distant memory. In addition to which my attention had by now turned to other women. As my power and influence grew, more women were drawn to me, and new trade deals meant sleeping with influential women. I even fathered some children in foreign lands. Let me tell you more about this now.

CHAPTER 59

The General Maximus Aurelius, His Wife, and Their Daughter

I had been invited to the home of a foreign general, Maximus Aurelius; we had just concluded a major trade deal and it was time to celebrate. His sophisticated dwellings, with their fine marbled floors, bore no relation to the primitive huts I was used to back home.

I was invited to take a bath with General Maximus Aurelius, his wife, and their young daughter. While bathing, we drank wine, ate fine grapes, and recalled the battles we had fought. They didn't fully believe me when I told them of the battles of my younger year, mocking me until I felt totally foolish.

"A dog you say," bawled the general, his eyes glinting, his voice laced with sarcasm. "We have been using such beasts for years. You don't feed them for five days; you bait them to attack the enemy and they rip into them. We've been doing this to barbarian tribes for years."

My other anecdotes, including the mission to kill Cervilius, were also met with great mirth - particularly the part of the old hag.

"Your land seems full of frauds and superstition," General Maximus Aurelius surmised, before pouring another glass of wine for himself. I had begun to wonder if such stories were just youthful fantasies, that I had been but a naïve boy until my more sophisticated commercial exploits. In the end, I had to laugh at myself - I didn't want to appear even more preposterous before the General and his lady folk.

The general's hospitality proved to be more than lavish.

He even offered me two fine slave girls to "entertain me" during the long night, which he said would be a cold one. I declined. I was somewhat weary from my travels and the mockery I had been at the receiving end of concerning my past, and I just wanted to be left alone. Truth be told, I was irked – the general had gone too far. However, my wish for solitude was not to be granted. I was drifting off to sleep when I felt a presence in my room.

"Can I join you, Mordred?" a sweet voice said.

Taken aback, I felt at first prone to reject the request, when eventually, through the darkness, I made out the form of the general's young daughter. She dropped her night robe and stood in front of me naked. What if the general heard voices and was stirred in the night? His daughter was young, and I imagined he would be very protective of her.

Reluctantly, I pulled back the covers and she gleefully joined me, giggling. Up to now she hadn't said a word to me. I had spotted her staring at me, observing me like I was some exotic bird in a cage. Despite my strong reservations, I succumbed to her charms easily. We were soon holding one another closely and kissing, and before long I found myself on top of her, hoping that the increasingly loud noises we were emitting wouldn't awaken the general.

After our lovemaking, she slipped out of bed and returned to her own chambers, while I managed to drift off into a rather laboured sleep.

Until for the second time that night, I was disturbed by a visitor. I assumed it was the young woman returning for another illicit love session. Much to my surprise, it wasn't the girl, but her mother. Following her daughter's routine, she let her night robe casually fall to the floor. I was speechless for a moment, but I lifted the covers to let her join me.

I whispered into her ear, "What are you doing?'

"I seek your body," she replied, unabashedly.

"What about your husband, Maximus Aurelius, what if he discovers us?"

"He won't," she replied confidently. "He has gone away on a mission and won't be back for a while. He's shown no interest in me since I bore him a daughter."

Without any shame she soon had me making love to her, as I'd done with her daughter. Like her daughter before her, she slunk out of my room.

There was no sign of the general in the morning. I went about my business in other parts of the country before returning home. I didn't return to this country for a while, but when I did, I was met with only cold disdain. I later discovered the reason for it: I had managed to get both mother and daughter pregnant, and General Maximus Aurelius, furious with me, had vowed to get his revenge and stop all trade with our tribe.

I turned angry and resentful towards the general. If perhaps I had overstepped, and abused the General's hospitality, I had also been almost violated by both women, who had forced themselves upon me. Putting an end to what had been a fruitful trading partnership seemed excessive on his part. I vowed he would be the one who would pay... not me. I quickly returned home and immediately called a war council, explaining that trade had stopped, and an invasion of our lands might even be planned as we spoke. I threw a little bit more oil on the fire by explaining that General Maximus Aurelius had mocked our gods and our culture.

CHAPTER 60

The Ambush

Rather than sending an army, I asked for money to purchase the services of some fierce mercenaries, some weaponry and just take a few of our top warriors. I didn't expect to do battle in the traditional way but would still defeat this General and his army. The council, although confused about my real motives, agreed to my request.

From one of my foreign sources, I learned that General Maximus Aurelius was away fighting a campaign, but would be returning in a matter of weeks, passing through a forest I could use to my advantage on his way.

I enlisted mercenaries, bought a range of weapons - light swords, large lances, and short narrow-bladed spears. The weaponry also included five fighting dogs trained to kill. I formed an alliance with another local tribe, which boosted our numbers and allowed me to use local knowledge of how to enact an ambush.

We discreetly camped in the forest, sharpened our weapons, and relayed skills and battle tactics to all, biding our time.

Finally, the moment arrived. The army, led by General Maximus Aurelius, could be seen and heard from afar, heading towards the place where we had set the ambush.

I soon spotted him on horseback, foot soldiers following behind him. The signal was raised and in no time, javelins rained down, as well as arrows from archers. I saw a javelin hit the General's horse and he was thrown to the ground. The darkness of the forest meant it was hard for the enemy to target our combatants.

The next onslaught was the dogs who, once unleashed, immediately set upon enemy soldiers. Their eyes were demonic, fiery embers. The dogs sprang at the soldiers, ripping at any naked flesh of arms or legs, and even necks.

The dogs caused the wanton chaos. I had heeded the advice of the General himself; the brutes hadn't been fed for five days and were ravenous and angry. The enemy's troops were spread about and disorganized. Our men jumped from their vantage points, from both sides screaming wildly as they began to engage in battle with the enemy, who were not trained to fight this way.

The battle seemed to be over quickly; many enemy bodies strewn on the mushy ground as the rain poured down. I went in search of General Maximus Aurelius and found him face down in the mud, a knife sticking out of his back. He was already long dead.

After this major victory, an army was gathered and we ravaged the country, taking anything, we could.

When I returned to my tribal settlement, with all the treasures I had accumulated, I was welcomed as a hero. I never thought about the two women I had impregnated, nor the offspring I had helped bring into this world. They were such a distant memory and I wondered if this episode had ever happened - I had been in a drunken stupor at the time.

What I was sure of was the four slave girls I was now sleeping with - those same girls I had discovered with Carvilius, the night I had entered his hut to chop his head off. I had demanded they be brought back to our settlement, as part of our agreement with the defeated tribe. I didn't intend to abuse them in the way Carvilius had. Indeed, I felt pity for them. And of course, I enjoyed the comfort of sleeping alongside them. I liked the warmth their naked bodies emitted on cold nights. I enjoyed picking one, or maybe two, to give me pleasure, massaging and caressing my body. In turn, I also liked to caress their bodies. There was no emotional attachment, it was purely about physical pleasure.

They were often sad when I left on another escapade in far-off lands. With my last success, I replicated the same strategy. If countries didn't offer favourable trading terms, I would make alliances with neighbouring tribes, defeat their armies, then strip the country of all its valuable resources. I was, far and wide, gaining a formidable reputation.

CHAPTER 61

An Encounter with a Princess

My reputation as a paramour was also growing. I became the lover of an Iberian princess, who had invited me to her palace.

When I arrived at her palace, I immediately noticed her hauntingly penetrating gaze. The princess was wearing a dress bedecked in jewels and an elaborate headdress, as well as long, shoulder-length, tassel-like earrings which swung when she moved her head. On her fingers were an array of rings, which glinted when she moved her hands.

"So, you are Mordred," she said. I didn't answer, just nodded. She looked me up and down, like I was some kind of God. Conversation was awkward between us; despite the large amounts of wine we had drunk.

After a time, a servant arrived to indicate it was dinner time. The food was unlike any I had previously experienced, razor clams, scallops, and chopped octopus with olive oil and paprika.

I ate a lot before she ushered me to sit alongside on her couch. She fed me figs, while musicians played their flutes, tambourines, and pipes. Monkeys even came in to perform a dance for my entertainment.

When suddenly, the princess clapped her hands and all the entertainers left at once. The doors opened and a muscular man entered, a wild cat on a lead who eyed me with disdain walking next to him. The animal's entrance seemed to please the princess.

"Cabra," purred the princess, "my sweet little lynx." She stroked the cat, who looked up at her affectionately.

"Mordred, you will do as I wish, or I will release Cabra. And I can assure you her claws are razor sharp and she has a nasty temper." The princess let out a little laugh to show she meant business.

I didn't reply, I was wondering how things would develop. I drew in the princess' strong aroma - a woody, rich scent. I had never encountered a woman such as her. A gong sounded. The lynx was led away, then in walked four muscular, tanned men dressed in only white loin cloths, carrying baskets full of scented petals.

The princess signalled to me to follow her with a flick of her hand. I duly followed her, as the four men scattered the sweet-smelling petals to make a path for us to follow. Eventually, we reached a large room glistening with candles in ornate candelabras.

In the centre of the room was a large bed with magnificent carvings. The four men discretely left the room. Two beautiful maids wearing simple white tunics entered and helped the princess undress behind a screen. As they did so, the princess called out.

"Mordred, I want you stripped and in my bed by the time I am finished with these maids." She was ordering me about as if I were a servant. She didn't know any different, he'd spent her entire life-giving orders. Slowly, I did as I was told and climbed under the thin covers. She ordered her maids to leave, which they did dutifully.

Her black hair, now let down, was so long it reached her hips. She was still wearing make-up, but was dressed in a simple white gown, which she gently let slip to the floor. She walked unashamed, totally naked, and joined me in bed.

"Kiss me, Mordred!" she ordered. Of course, I did as I was ordered. Soon I was on top of her, and we were making love. When we had finished, she called out to a servant to bring a flask of wine. We drank from gold goblets. I seemed to fascinate her. She asked me about my tribe's beliefs and culture and laughed at times when I told her. She said her life was at times boring and that she sought adventures – I suppose this is what I was, an adventure.

We spent the night together and as light began to stream into the room, she told me groggily to dress and leave. I had been dismissed like one of her servants, been treated like some kind of plaything and felt defiled. I was not a nobleman, and I knew that if I had been, I would not have been involved in such situations and would have been treated with respect.

CHAPTER 62

An Excursion to Eastern Europe

A little time later, I had an encounter with a woman from Easten Europe. She was a great beauty called Estera. Her husband, Kazik, was well-known in the region, as a landowner and warrior.

After an excursion, he had come home to discover his younger brother Hipolet had met a young girl and the two of them had fallen in love and hastily decided to marry.

When Kazik first met his new sister-in-law Estera, he fell immediately under her spell. He had never been in the company of a woman so beautiful and charming. He immediately vowed to have the girl for himself. In his mind, Hipolet was weak and undeserving, whereas he was a warrior with impressive credentials.

He was surprised Hepolet had managed to woo the girl, as the lad could usually be found drinking ale with his friends and begging his older brother for money to sustain his decadent lifestyle.

Kazik believed his younger brother was using this marriage as way of gaining favour and tapping into the wealth of Estera's family, who were of a rich and notable family, and owned much land in the region.

The night before the wedding, Kazik came to Estera's house. She was surprised to see Kazik. He told her he wanted to speak to her alone, concerning a "rather delicate matter". But before they got down to discussing the serious business at hand, he suggested they try some wine he had procured especially for the wedding. Estera was a bit fearful of Kazik - Hipolet's older brother was a serious man whereas Hipolet was playful, and he made her laugh.

The first gulps of wine were drunk in silence. Then they talked about how she and Hipolet had met. Kazik had seduced many women and was loath to devote himself to just one, when there were so many beautiful ones around. But Estera was different - in awe of him whilst besotted with Hipolet. It was time for Kazik to force the issue.

"You can't marry my brother," he blurted out. Estera stared at him in silence, taking in what he had just said. "Why ever not?" she asked, pulling a face before defiantly adding, "we are to marry tomorrow."

"Listen," said Kazik brusquely, "there are many things you don't know about my brother. Those moments when he is prone to insanity. His rages, usually determined by the moon."

The girl was still unmoved, so Kazik added, "He contracted a disease by sleeping with many whores encountered on his travels."

Hipolet had indeed talked of his travels with Estera - but obviously not about the disease, or the whores.

"He is such a sweet man, your brother, how can you say such terrible things?"

"I am afraid the truth can often prove to be very ugly," Kazik said, noting the girl was now concerned.

"I have had to save him and the honour of our family many times, and I would hate to see your family associated with any kind of scandal."

"But it will be a scandal if I don't marry him tomorrow. Many noble families have been invited to the ceremony."

"But you can still marry, sweet Estera," Kazik said cryptically.

"How so?" asked the innocent girl.

"You will marry me. We will explain that the undependable Hipolet has fled during the night and I, Kazik, his honourable brother, have dutifully agreed to replace him."

The young girl looked downcast. Kazik encouraged her to drink more wine. However, at one point she began to weep, which Kazik used as an excuse to comfort her, putting his muscular arms around her like a father protecting a daughter in a wild storm. Estera didn't appear to want to fight him off. She had lost her father not long before, and it was Hipolet who had consoled her then. But he had lied to her - he was a man with a double personality, not that she had witnessed his other side. She began to feel groggy and even more helpless. Kazik's hands began to wander, caressing her long blonde hair.

Audaciously, he began to fondle one of her breasts. They kissed, at first awkwardly but then with an unanticipated surge of passion.

Kazik had completed his mission to sabotage his brother's wedding and steal his bride's heart, and he could now take his leave.

Now he had to deal with his brother and a devious plan began to emerge in his head, a plan that pleased him so much he started to laugh out loud. Night-time was over and there wasn't much time before the ceremony was due to start.

There was nobody about - all the servants were sleeping. He headed to his brother's sleeping quarters but found them empty, his bed undisturbed. His brother was obviously elsewhere - a place where he could often be found entertaining his friends. Indeed, Kazik found him slumped on the floor of his favourite drinking haunt, surrounded by a strong smell of alcohol and urine, goblets half-filled with wine spread about that suggested a last party before the wedding.

Hipolet had doubtlessly toasted his future bride's health too many times and even his drinking friends had got bored of his drunken antics and left.

Kazik shook Hipolet to rouse him. "Come, brother. Let's go for a little walk. Light is breaking, and a walk would do you good. You seem in no fit state for getting married."

His brother didn't respond, just mumbling and groaning as he was being lifted off the floor.

Kazik had to support his brother, who kept stumbling and cursing as they trudged to the nearby woods. Hipolet was barely conscious, and unaware of what was happening. The brothers followed a meandering path, brambles occasionally hindering their progress, as a light drizzle started to fall.

"Where are we going?" Hipolet managed to ask.

"You'll see my dear Hipolet," Kazik replied.

At one point, Hipolet stumbled forward and started retching - a consequence of his reckless drinking. The wind and the drizzle grew stronger, and this seemed to rouse Hipolet.

"I want to go back," he moaned, his voice now clearer and filled with frustration, as his brother dragged him deeper in the woods. Hipolet had hardly ever ventured into the woods - he had never been interested in the outdoor pursuits like his brother, who was a keen hunter and had killed aurochs, wild bison, and elks.

Kazik sensed his brother's resistance and gripped him strongly by the arm, dragging him more forcefully.

"Brother, what are you doing?" demanded Hipolet, increasingly concerned as the woods seemed to get denser, dank and threatening; even the cries of the wild animals and the flutter of birds' wings disturbed him.

Suddenly, Kazik pushed his brother to the mushy ground. Out of the sack hanging on his back, he produced some cord. Hipolet didn't put up much resistance, too shocked to move. Kazik tightly bound Hipolet's hands and marched away from the path towards a tree with a thin trunk. With another piece of chord, he tied up Hipolet's ankles. Finally, with what was left of the rope, he secured Hipolet to the tree. Wolves and other wild animals who would surely find Hipolet an easy prey - that's what Kazik was counting on.

"Enjoy your wedding day, dear brother," said Kazik in a sardonic laugh.

Hipolet didn't answer; he was too busy wailing with desperation as the rain began to come down even stronger and the wicked wind from the east seemed to get the temperature a degree or two colder. Kazik quickly walked back from the woods, hoping nobody would notice him, and went to his bedroom to get a few hours' sleep.

In the morning, he put on his finest clothes and jewellery, which signified his importance as both a nobleman and a heroic warrior. He heard some commotion - people had finally notice Hipolet's absence.

Kazik called a meeting. Guests and family members gathered in the hallway, intrigued. In a commanding voice, not that too dissimilar from that he frequently used with his men before engaging in battle, he explained the situation.

"As you all know, my brother Hipolet is due to marry in a few hours."

On waking up this morning I discovered that my

brother had been sleeping with prostitutes under this very roof the night before he was to marry a sweet innocent maiden. When I confronted him about his disgraceful behaviour, he said he no longer wished to marry and wished to go travel the world. I told him his actions would bring disgrace to our family. On further thought and with my brother's consent, it is I, Kazik, who will step in for my disgraced brother and marry sweet Estera."

There was a collective sigh of shock from all those present.

"I will shortly be visiting her family to explain the situation and ask if I can replace my degenerate brother." Kazik marched off, leaving family and friends to mull over this incredible turn of events. He was soon back home, a triumphant grin on his face.

"All is arranged," he trumpeted. "The ceremony will be going ahead."

Indeed, he had been most convincing with Estera's family. Her younger brother, an aspiring warrior, was now head of the family and Kazik had promised him a fine career, along with pledging a lot of fine jewellery and horses - much of which he had acquired on his campaigns. He clearly had far more to offer than his younger brother, who had disgraced himself and proved unworthy of Estera's love.

Her family had suffered a turn in their fortunes following the father's sudden demise, and Kazik was just what they needed to be on the way up again.

Estera's feelings on the matter were not taken into consideration, but her family's prospects were.

What had Hipolet even had to offer in comparison to Kazik? His witty words, his jesting, nothing else.

The wedding proceeded. Family and friends stood in

a circle, looking at Kazik and his beautiful wife kneeling in front the altar holding symbols for the four elements, fire represented with a red candle, air symbolized with incense, water, and earth.

The young bride wore a crown of flowers while the groom, had reluctantly accepted to put a crown of ivy on his head. Estera carried a bouquet of herbs to ward off evil spirits as well as flowers symbolising her love for Kazik.

The circle was blessed, and the goddesses were called upon. Some beautiful verses were read, and these two almost total strangers officially became man and wife - although there wasn't much joy, let alone love, emanating from them.

Kazik and Estera's hands were bound by a woven thread, and just before the giving of rings, the binding was slipped off with the knot still intact, signifying they would always be bound together in marriage.

The congregation walked back to Estera's home. Some flowers were thrown at the newlyweds, who walked in an awkward silence.

The feast that followed at least brought about some merriment. Kazik and his bride Estera drank the bridal ale that had been meant for Estera and his missing brother.

Estera presented the bridal ale to Kazik in a drinking vessel made of birch burr and dedicated her own first sip to a goddess of fate, while Kazik dedicated his to the gods of war and thunder.

The musicians Hipolet had commissioned were now in place, and dancing soon began. Kazik felt obligated to dance with his young bride, who occasionally smiled but was still too much in shock.

The feast included sweet bread, which would be

offered with prayers to the gods before being given to Kazik and Estera, followed by a broth and a dish of herring. The drinking, eating, and dancing went on late into the night.

Having had little sleep the night before and bored by the proceedings, Kazik led his young bride away and despite both being weary, he still managed to make brief, perfunctory love to her, after which they both fell asleep.

The feast cut short by the absence of the newlyweds; the wedding guests started to disperse. Many reflected the day had been a strange and unnatural one.

The next morning, Kazik left the bridal bed early and went about his usual business, a pattern he would proceed to follow from then on, ignoring his wife or absent due to urgent matters requiring his attention.

And what of Hipolet? Helpless, isolated, in fear of being attacked by wolves or other predators, he remained alive for days. Of course, he now felt hatred for his brother as well as sorrow since he had been denied the chance to marry sweet Estera. Why had Kazik done this terrible thing? What if Kazik had taken away from him the one person he had ever truly loved?

Was he to die alone in the woods, from thirst or hunger, or perhaps from the cold bitter nights? Sometimes he would lose consciousness. Once he even imagined he saw Estera, walking daintily by herself, picking flowers in the woods, sweetly smiling to herself. But this was just his imagination, playing a cruel trick on him. When reality crept back in, he felt even more distant from her. He was beginning to realize death was close when he heard voices. Despite his weakness, he cried out. He was almost inaudible, but somehow, his cries for help didn't go unnoticed.

CHAPTER 63

The Camp

Two women, holding wicker baskets, both wearing decorative head scarfs, their faces etched with furrows were staring at him, totally bemused and laughing at him and at his predicament. He feared they might leave him alone once again when suddenly one of them produced a knife from the basket she was carrying and cut the rope and chords, setting him free. He was unable to stand up and had no idea how long he had been left attached to the tree. All he knew what that he urgently needed food.

One of the women shouted out a name, repeating it several times until a man appeared. A conversation ensued in a language Hepolet couldn't understand.

"Help me," he managed to say, his eyes imploring them.

The man managed to haul Hipolet up and demanded the taller of the two women help him to support the weight of Hipolet. Progress was slow, until they reached a small cart, which seem to belong to the man. With great effort, Hipolet was heaved onto the cart and taken away to a large clearing where their people had set up camp. Hipolet drew in the smell of smoke, as fires were heating something up in huge cauldrons.

People approached the cart and looked at Hipolet in bemusement. The cart came to a standstill and a large man came out of his tent, having been alerted by the commotion created by Hipolet's arrival. He looked cautiously at Hipolet. Another conversation developed, which Hepolet was again totally excluded from. The large man re-entered his tent and came back with a beautiful young girl - perhaps his daughter.

She smiled at Hipolet, before asking in a heavily accented voice, "What is your name?"

"Hipolet Zimneoczy ," Hipolet replied.

His name seemed to arouse further animated conversation.

"You are from a noble family," the young girl said, her eyes lit up and a beaming smile spreading across her face.

"Yes, that is true I suppose," Hipolet answered.

"And yet you were found bound to a tree. Why?" the young girl asked.

"My brother did this. I was about to marry and the night before the wedding, he led me into the woods and left me for dead."

The young girl translated what Hipolet had told her to the group, who in turn roared with laughter, as if they had just heard the funniest thing ever. Hipolet looked on stony-faced, failing to share their mirth. "Most sorry," the young girl continued, "but why would a brother do such a thing? What is his name?"

"Kazik Zimneoczy," Hipolet replied.

Animated conversations started as soon as he had said his brother's name.

"Your brother is a bad man," the young girl said.

"Why do you say this?" Hipolet asked, bemused.

"His men recently killed two of ours, and he has vowed to drive us off this land, although we cause him no harm."

It seemed Hipolet had been discovered by a travelling

tribe involved in a feud with his brother. At last, his luck had turned.

"You need to eat and drink," said the young girl with that provocative smile of hers. Hipolet was delighted to hear these words, such was his hunger and weakness he would have eaten anything that was presented to him. He was taken to a tent. Shortly after, the young girl returned with a generous plate filled with a stew made of beef pork and game.

Hipolet suspected the deer had been poached from Kazik's considerable herd and the beef from his herd of cows. The pork was possibly from wild pigs caught in the woods. Whatever, the plate of food was very welcome. Accompanying the plate of food was a large morsel of bread, which Hipolet attacked like a ravenous wolf. The young girl also brought a vessel filled with elderberry juice. Once he had finished, she left him. He had barely slept during his ordeal, so he quickly drifted off to sleep.

He dreamed of Estera, kneeling in front of an altar. His drinking friends were in a circle, surrounding her, they were laughing hysterically, some of them dancing a ridiculous dance. Suddenly, he became aware of himself. He was being dragged on his back with a rope, on a horse ridden by Kazik. When Kazik reached the altar, he dismounted. He bowed to all those in the circle, as if receiving some great acclaim. Suddenly, he produced a whip and cracked it on the ground sending the horse with Hipolet attached careering away.

Hipolet woke up and heard the distant sounds of voices, clapping and tambourine, with a melody provided by a flute. The entrance to his tent was parted and the young girl appeared, sweat pouring down her face. She was wearing a beautiful, pleated skirt and a tight low-cut blouse with a V-neck showing off her ample cleavage. It was obvious to Hipolet she had been dancing.

"I heard you call out," she said in an anxious voice. "Is everything all right?"

"It is kind of you to be concerned, but it was simply a dream," replied Hipolet as the music seemed to gather momentum. Hipolet regretted he had missed the chance to watch her dance.

"I see," said the young roamer before leaving Hipolet to his thoughts. With the distant music assisting him, he drifted back to sleep.

The following days were monotonous, with many lonely hours spent by himself and interludes of the young girl bringing him food and drink to make him stronger. Eventually, he had enough strength to haul himself up. With the help of the young traveller, he managed to make a few steps forward. She advised caution, as she said he would require more time before he could walk unaided.

One morning he dared ask her what her name was.

"Yoska," she replied.

"Yoska, you have saved me. You are kind and I thank you deeply."

"There are many here who might do you harm, but my father listens to me, and I have asked that you are protected."

"Who is your father?" asked Hipolet.

"He is Menowin. He is a tribal chieftain."

"That makes you a princess," said Hipolet.

"That maybe so, but it is just in my blood. I am not a leader like my father."

"Your father has no kingdom," suggested Hipolet.

"He roams where he wishes across many lands. He is part of wide family, which will come together shortly as we are about to have a large gathering of kin."

Indeed, Hipolet had noted some new arrivals, when he glimpsed out of the tent he was confined to. He had heard tents being pitched.

He was given the opportunity to test his strength and see if he could take a few steps unaided. Yoska even convinced her father to let him eat with the large group that were now assembled in the woods.

After the meal, which included rabbit stew, combined with ham, onions, mushrooms and stock, all of it seasoned with marjoram, thyme, salt and pepper, the celebrations began as musicians started playing hypnotic melodies. When the party seemed to be reaching its peak, Yoska, who hadn't participated much up to now suddenly appeared, accompanied by another young and equally beautiful girl. It appeared they were a double act, but for what? Hipolet wondered. There was an expectation among the crowd gathered to watch them. A large wooden table was rotated so that it was standing upright, and the other traveller girl stood in front of it.

Yoska was then blindfolded. She took out six knives, projecting the first one to land to the left of the girls' head, then a second to the right. A massive cheer greeted each successful throw. The next two landed to the left and right of the girl's hips and the last two to the left and right of the girl's knees. Each throw was achieved with great precision. She took off her blindfold and reaped the applause.

A man threw a cabbage up in the air and she split it in two, with another precise throw. With two quick throws, she managed to embed the knives in a pumpkin that had been launched in the air by the same man. She seemed able to hit any target, either moving or static. Everyone including Hipolet was impressed by her incredible talent.

Once Yoska had finished entertaining everybody with her knife throwing, she turned their attention to dancing, along with her lookalike assistant who had risked her life during the knife-throwing spectacle. The two moved gracefully and joyfully, while occasionally lifting their long skirts. Those gathered round sung and clapped or banged tambourines. Hipolet looked on in awe.

At one point, exhaustion got the better of him and he shuffled back to his tent, where he fell asleep while the music and clapping continued long into the night.

The next morning, he was surprised when Yoska came to visit him. He could fend for himself, and was less dependent on her kindness, apart from the provision of food.

"What did you think about last night?" Yoska asked with a sweet smile, her eyes glistening.

"It was incredible. You have such talent, both your knife throwing and your dancing. How did you learn?"

"From my father," she replied, "he taught me from a young age how to use a knife. I can fight with a knife as well as any man."

"I don't doubt it," Hipolet replied.

"Can you fight with a knife?" Yoska asked Hipolet.

"Not at all," answered Hipolet.

Unlike his brother, he'd never been involved in any kind of fighting, apart from drunken brawls.

"Well, I shall show you," said Yoska.

"That would be great," said Hipolet, imagining this meant he would get to spend some time with her, as well as learning useful skills that might come useful in the future. Yoska promised to return shortly. Hipolet was pleased she did as she had promised and in no time, the first session had begun.

Hipolet felt strange holding a knife. His efforts to follow her instructions were poor at first. Equally, he felt slow and sluggish, far from capable of any kind of over-exertion. He felt embarrassed by his paltry efforts.

Yoska was a patient teacher and seemed determined to make her student learn the basics of handling a knife and basic fighting skills. After a few days, the rewards of labour became apparent, as Hipolet became more accomplished. He hadn't drunk a drop of alcohol since the day before what should have been his wedding day.

Yoska also taught Hipolet how to throw a knife, by getting him to throw as accurately as possible at targets. One morning, as they were in the midst of one of their sessions, there was a commotion. A crowd seemed gathered around an old woman who was shrieking in pain and in great anguish. Yoska raced away to see what was happening.

Later she told Hipolet what had happened. The old lady had been searching for wild onions, garlic and chives. She had been spotted by one of Kazik's men. Kazik had had her whipped with a horse whip. Luckily, she had been discovered by another person who had brought her back to the camp as quickly as possible. "Did you know this is ancient tribal land?" asked Yoska.

"I never knew that" answered Hipolet.

"We were hounded out, father told me all, and now we are unable to roam where our ancestors did."

A meeting was called, tempers were flaring. Some kind of revenge was required. Others might even join to fight Kazik. One person who had serious reasons to seek revenge… Hipolet.

He knew exactly what would hurt Kazik more than anything. Kazik had a favourite horse named Horka, which he had ridden into battle, rode when hunting, and who had saved his life on several occasions. He adored the horse in the same way a parent might love his own offspring. Although it might be difficult to steal this fine horse, it would hurt Kazik more than anything. Kazik had the horse guarded even during the night. It would take a carefully planned and daring raid to deprive Kazik of his greatest possession. A group of ten of the finest horse thieves were given the responsibility of completing the mission and a clever plan was hatched. Hipolet tried to pass on as much information as he could to help the men on their dangerous mission.

Their first task was to incapacitate the guards. While the guards were checking on the horses, a man left a vessel of ale brewed to produce a strong level of alcohol. The vessel was left close to the fire where the guards had been sitting to keep warm. It was a cold night and when they returned, they were delighted and surprised to find the gift. Soon they were swigging the ale down and in no time they were drunk. The camp's men came up from behind them and put sacks over their heads. The men were defenceless.

Two of the thieves were excellent at handling horses, and although Horka was agitated at first, they managed to attach a rope round his neck and lead him away. The two guards, in a drunken stupor and in a state of shock, were then placed where the favourite animal had been staying.

When the first successful raid was completed, another was immediately planned to rub further salt into the Kazik's wounds. A party was quickly assembled to round up some of his fine herd of deer. It was another successful raid, which would furthermore provide for a fine feast.

Rumours started to circulate about the audacious theft of Kazik's valued horse and much-admired herd of deer.

I, Mordred, was in the area, travelling with twelve of my finest warriors while enjoying the hospitality of a local chieftain. I was familiar with Kazik - not that I had had met him before. I was told he had recently married a beautiful young woman and had a reputation for being a ruthless warrior.

I had met Menowin and, despite the communication barrier, we had struck up an unlikely friendship. Menowin was known for being able to drink more horns of ale than anybody else. He had a raucous laugh and a beautiful daughter. I found myself tempted to pay Menowin a visit to see if I could assist him in any way. I still owed him for a service, for he had introduced me to a powerful fur trader. I was told that Kazik would not stand for the effrontery and would surely be coming to the camp to get his beloved horse back home.

When I arrived at the traveller's camp, I was greeted with a great bear hug from Menowin. We made awkward attempts at conversation and ended up roaring with laughter at our mutual lack of understanding. I noticed that Menowin's beautiful daughter seemed to be with a young man I'd never seen before and was told he was no other than Kazik's brother Hipolet.

With my limited knowledge of the local dialect he managed to convey to me what had happened.

I listened in amazement. the whole of the camp seemed in a celebratory mood. I feared that could soon change if Kazik were to attack.

I tried to relay my fears to Menowin. Did he have any plans for how to repel an attack or indeed to stop the threat posed by Kazik. He just roared with laughter, as was his way.

There was an immediate need to fortify the camp and send away any women and children. There needed to be strategy, a way to surprise Kazik. Perhaps another raid, this time to decimate as many of his men as possible. Menowin seemed unimpressed. He was not as used to war as I was. Finally, he pointed at Hipolet.

"We have him, he is our greatest weapon."

Even Hipolet was taken aback.

"Also, we have Kazik's favourite horse. All we need to do is lure him here," Menowin said with eyes that looked like they could see the future.

I was unconvinced but listened to Menowin's ideas.

A message was sent to Kazik to come to the woods alone at an appointed time if he wanted to recover his horse. Menowin's plan had its risks. Would Kazik come alone, or would he bring others to protect him?

Fortunately, he did as he was instructed.

A signal was given that Kazik was approaching. The woods were surrounded by an eerie, thick fog.

The tribe, as well as myself and some of my warriors, were hidden in different vantage points, waiting in silence, full of dread and uncertainty.

"I've come for my horse!" Kazik said in an authoritative voice. There was no immediate response. Suddenly, a figure appeared as if from nowhere, enveloped in thick fog. The figure was hooded, dressed in a white tunic. The face and hair were white, as if it was a spectre returned from the other world.

Suddenly, the figure spoke. "You have come for your horse, and I have come for revenge, brother."

Kazik shuddered. "I had left you for dead," he said, his voice not as assured as usual.

"You thought you had seen the last of me, but it is you, brother, who will suffer," Hipolet, said with surprising confidence.

"Don't be a fool, brother. You have never fought a battle in your sad life," responded Kazik, smirking.

"Things have changed, brother, and it is I who will prevail," shouted Hipolet, full of bravado.

The fog engulfed Hipolet again. It was as if the Gods had created the perfect conditions for Menowin's plan. When he reappeared, Hipolet was holding a knife.

"Don't be ridiculous, brother, I'll cut you down in seconds. You don't stand a chance," Kazik bawled.

Without warning, Hipolet threw the knife. The throw wasn't as accurate as he would have hoped, however he fortuitously managed to slice off one of Kazik's ears. Kazik screamed in pain. Blood streamed to the ground.

"Brother, take a knife," said Hipolet as his brother tried to regain his composure.

All those hidden away in their vantage points were taken by surprise. Hipolet was given the challenge of killing his brother, not obliging him with a fair fight.

The two men ran towards each other. Kazik managed to swerve away from Hipolet's opening lunge. Kazik was far stronger than his brother, so Hipolet would only succeed if he employed some of the tricks he had learned from Yoska. It was also obvious he would have to defeat his older brother soon because Kazik certainly would have more durability. So far, there had been no serious blows.

With a sudden jab, Hipolet managed a jab, which resulted in a wound to Kazik's left arm.

His injuries far from incapacitated Kazik but were still enough to impair his ability to fight with his usual vigour.

Suddenly, Kazik drew his sword and severely injured Hipolet. Using the force of a mighty kick, he sent Hipolet flying to the ground. Standing over his brother who was now lying helpless on his back, he lifted his sword upwards and with all his might, stabbed his brother's abdomen. He pulled out the sword and held it triumphantly up in the air. Blood from the brother was everywhere.

"Now bring me my horse!" cried Kazik, having triumphed over his adversary.

By the time he had finished the word horse, a knife came flying from behind him and lodged in his back.

He fell to his knees, before lurching forward to the ground. Soon, he was breathing his last. Yoska walked towards him to see how accurate and incisive her throw had been. Once she was certain he was dead, she went over to Hipolet's body, held on to his lifeless corpse tightly and began to weep violently.

It was plain to see for all that she'd been in love with him. Perhaps she blamed herself for his demise - perhaps she could have trained him better.

Yoska's father walked over to her and gently pulled

her away, still mourning her great loss. She was covered in his blood, tears streaming down her face, wailing his name over and over again. Hipolet's death took away the shine of what could have been a glorious night.

I was saddened by the young man's death, but I still had plans now that Kazik was dead. There were riches to be had. Without any qualms, I took a knife and cut off the head of the dead military man.

With the warriors I had with me, a couple of fighting dogs and a few volunteers from the tribe, we set off for a surprise attack on Kazik's men.

Kazik had imagined he could easy retrieve his horse - he was only up against a band of travellers, after all. His men were not adequately ready for our sudden, dramatic assault and were shocked into stupor as I brazenly displayed Kazik's head.

Some quickly ran away, while others tried to put up some semblance of resistance, despite their weariness and the ferocity of the unanticipated attack.

Finally, we overcame Kazik's men, who were no match for my fearsome warriors. We spared their lives on the understanding they would leave Kazik's land as well as leave the nomadic tribe to stay on their ancient land. I returned to the camp with my group of warriors for some sleep.

Drifting off to sleep, I could still hear Yoska's moans of anguish.

The next day, I took my small band of warriors to see what spoils could be taken from Kazik's estate. The village seemed eerily deserted. Eventually we entered a room where a beautiful young girl was sitting serenely.

"Your husband is dead," I said to the young woman.

She didn't flinch or recoil in shock. She just sat and stared into space.

Finally, she responded, "I heard he has been slain."

To reinforce the point, I lifted his head from a sack and tossed it to the ground. She stared at it for a while, but her face never showed any emotion.

"He was a cruel man. It was inevitable he would die a terrible death."

"He killed his own brother," I said.

"I heard this as well," she said, this time showing signs of sadness.

She then proceeded to tell me the whole story. She told me that she was happy that her husband was dead, that it lifted a great burden from her shoulders.

"Tell me about yourself," she asked me. I told her about my life. She sat listening, nodding at me from time to time. For some reason, we seemed to enjoy each other's company.

I explained that my warriors were seeking some kind of recompense for their toils. She said her husband had a large quantity of furs they could take, as well as weapons. She immediately proceeded to show them where they could find her dead husband's possessions.

"What is your name?" she asked.

"Mordred," I replied.

"Well, Mordred, I would like to invite you to dine with me. I could get some of the remaining servants to prepare something for us." I was surprised by her unlikely offer, but accepted it nonetheless.

The warriors returned laden with Kazik's effects. I told them I would see them back at the camp and that we would be returning home the following day. The food provided by Estera was unusual to me, honey-braised bear paws served with horseradish-flavoured salad, accompanied by goblets of mead.

When we had finished eating, a sadness entered her eyes.

"Kazik was a brutal and uncaring lover," she said before lifting the hem of her tunic, showing bruises all over her shapely legs.

"But you, Mordred, would be a sweet, benevolent one, I am sure."

I didn't reply. I felt strangely drawn to her, despite only having known her but a short time.

The sadness soon led to tears, as she reflected on the cruelty that had befallen her in the recent past. She lifted her tunic over her head and stood before me naked. I quickly disrobed and soon we were together in a tight clench, her tears dampening my chest. Our lovemaking proved soothing to her, and soon we drifted away, our bodies still gripped together, inseparable.

In the morning, she seemed anxious. A glorious night had ended, and a question plagued her mind.

"Mordred, please don't leave me here. I have nothing here. I want you to take me with you. I want to live with you, back to your country. I never want to be parted from you, please dear Mordred."

She spoke in a desperate, pleading voice. I was certainly mesmerised by her beauty and felt a strange need to protect her. It was like I was not in control of my own will, for I would usually have immediately dismissed such a request.

"I will take you with me," I replied after a while. She hugged me even more strongly, and tears welled up in her eyes.

She gathered a few possessions and soon we were

making our way to the camp.

Her presence was met with surprise, some people furtively whispering behind our backs. I gathered my men and said my farewells to Menowin and his daughter, who was still grief-stricken, and we made our way to the coast before boarding a boat destined for our homeland. The journey was difficult, and the boat was churned about in rough seas.

CHAPTER 64

A Sudden Disappearance

When we approached land, something incredible happened. Suddenly, a dense mist descended and shrouded our boat. Everybody's vision was obscured, and we couldn't even see one another. If this continued, we might hit some rocks. We tried to light torches, but there was nothing we could do to improve the situation.

When the mist finally lifted, almost as quickly as it had come upon us, we discovered that Estera was no longer aboard and had vanished. If she had fallen into the water, we would have surely heard a splash and her screams for help. I was distraught. It was like she had never existed, except her possessions were still on board, the only evidence remaining of her existence. She had been calmly sleeping, while the men rowed the boat ever closer to the shoreline, but now, inexplicably, she was gone. I tossed her possessions into the sea, and we continued the journey, mystified at how this could come to pass.

CHAPTER 65

Power Struggle

Back home, the settlement was growing larger, with more and more huts being built to accommodate everybody. Olc was coming to the end of his life and leadership had been spread among different parties. And with it, constant power struggles.

Although I was often away, I had managed to earn the respect of the tribe. However, the younger members of the tribe who were unfamiliar with some of my feats and triumphs had their own ambitions.

With Olc's life ebbing away, it was decided that there should be a meeting followed by a vote to decide on who would be taking his place. I had always thought of myself as the heir apparent, as the one who had changed the tribe's fortunes. I had won so many battles, and travelled far and wide, making great discoveries. I had started to trade with other tribes and kingdoms. I was also sure Olc would favour me. After all, had I not cut off Cervilius' head?

Four possible replacements for Olc emerged at the meeting. A large crowd gathered to listen to what each of them had to say. They spoke of the battles they had fought in, the treasures they had gathered.

When my time came, I stood up. "Nobody in this room can claim to have done more for this tribe," I began.

"But you have been almost absent for many years. You have lost contact with this tribe. You are like a stranger to many," a young man shouted disdainfully. I barely knew this youth and was irked by his impudence.

"How dare you!" responded an elderly tribe member, who had known me since I was a boy, adding, "You are talking about the great Mordred, a hero of our tribe. The man who killed Carvilius in his own bed."

"Many things have changed here since those times," declared a still beardless young man who looked like he was barely out of his mother's arms.

I continued, "I will happily forego my trips to foreign lands and instead will conquer and unite tribes here in our homeland. I will rule not as a chieftain, but as a ruler of all."

This remark was met with roars of approval. The tide was turning my way.

Orc survived through the long winter, but one morning an announcement was made that he had passed into the next world. His passing was met with sadness. It was said that he spent his final hours with Milucrah, who had helped him along his final journey, and that he had talked about me, Mordred. My destiny, he had said, was unfulfilled, and I would make a great leader.

And so I, Mordred emerged as the new chieftain. I set about the task of augmenting my tribe's power and influence in the region. Money gained from foreign escapades was invested into hiring mercenaries and acquiring horses and chariots as well as spears and other weapons.

The tribe began to build its own assets. Rather than taking rewards, as had been done in the past, local chieftains were slain after defeat, along with the hierarchy of the vanquished tribe, then the tribe given the choice of joining ours or having their settlements burnt to the ground and possessions taken from them.

CHAPTER 66

Keeping The Order

Governing an ever-increasing area proved difficult. Any signs of rebellion had to be quickly quashed. A severe winter had also brought about a lack of food. Accompanied by five of my warriors, I went to visit a man who had been steeling cattle from us, and who was living outside our lands.

The man was known to be of volatile temper, and his family were feared in the region. As chieftain, I was expected to deal with him, bring him back to the settlement, where he would be brought to justice. The task proved harder than I had anticipated. He claimed he was only trying to provide for his family, that he had taken back what had belonged to him, that a neighbour had bad-mouthed him to get him punished. However, he eventually started cursing us, telling us to leave his abode.

His family also joined in the tirade of curses. His wife was a particularly abrasive and ugly woman, with a thick mesh of jet-black hair, long and jutting out in all directions. She was missing some teeth, and her eyes weren't symmetrical, one bulging more than the other and looking like it was about to pop out of her skull at any moment. She was covered in warts and pimples and stank of rancid vegetables and stale urine.

By contrast, her daughters seemed surprisingly beautiful, despite their sallow faces. The pleasantness of their looks couldn't mask the fact that they had vicious tongues and a vile attitude. They both ogled me and sneered when I spoke, passing sarcastic remarks. I tried to explain that if the man came willingly with us, he would be able to present his case. And if he was declared innocent, he would be set free. Such logic seemed lost on the man and his family.

Suddenly his wife, armed with a knife, ran towards one of my warriors, jabbing him in the shoulder. The oldest daughter grabbed a piece of wood from the fire and waved it about, causing the smoke to obscure our vision and giving the man time to bolt.

"After him!" I shouted, but the man was quick. Some people living nearby came to his aid and fights broke out, which allowed the man to get further away.

The man seemed to be heading towards our horses. He let them go with the help of another man, apart from one he climbed on. I launched a spear, which embedded itself into the man's back, making him scream in agony. It was a fortuitous hit, as if it had been directed by the gods. Through the gloom and smoke of the cattle thief's hut, I had suddenly spotted a spear. Where it had come from, I had no idea, but I had spontaneously picked it up. I had used such a weapon in battle in the past, but never from such a great distance.

I ran towards the severely injured man, wrenched out the spear and pulled him to the ground before thrusting my sword into his chest repeatedly. Then my warriors and I proceeded to destroy the settlement, setting fire to the huts. The impudence of his family had to be punished, as one of my warriors had been badly injured.

However, we spared the cattle thief's daughters. We would take them back to our settlement, where they would live as slaves.

CHAPTER 67

Precarious Return

The return journey was going to be hazardous, as it would take place during night-time and on foot, as the only remaining horse carried the wounded warrior. The journey was made even more painful by the wails of the two young girls - perhaps we should have simply left them behind.

Darkness set in quickly. We stopped for food and refreshments in readiness for the final part of our journey, which would involve going through large woods. As we reached the woods, we found ourselves surrounded by twelve men.

"What do we have here?" sneered one of the men, while another added, "It's late to be passing through these parts."

We were outnumbered and seemingly at the mercy of these malevolent men.

It crossed my mind to offer the girl, in exchange for peaceful passage. Other than this, I would have to take on these men with the help of the four fit warriors I had with me.

Out of the darkness another figure approached. She walked slowly and was bent over - the old hag was back. She addressed the men who were confronting us, "Threatening these men, are ya? Not very honourable when ladies are present."

"What of it, old hag? Be on your way, or we'll do some harm to you as well."

"I don't think so," said the old hag with surprising confidence.

Our antagonists were in no mood to listen to an old

crone and after a signal from their leader, they dashed towards us, weapons raised. They had only gone a few paces when each in turn let out a shriek of pain before falling to the ground, writhing in agony.

On closer inspection, I realised that thick brambles were wrapped around their ankles, razor-sharp thorns embedded deeply into their flesh.

I once again felt indebted to the old hag, but when I looked for her, she seemed to have vanished.

"Come on, let's get a move on," I ordered my men, leaving those who had threatened us to their own devices. As we moved on, we heard a dog snarling, followed by men screaming as they were being mercilessly attacked by the savage beast. We continued our journey, still bewildered by what had happened. Of course, I had encountered similar situations before, and I had met the old hag before - although not for many years.

When we arrived home in the early hours of the morning, no one was about apart from Milucrah, who approached us. "You have a wounded soldier, I see."

I explained how he had been attacked.

"I will take care of him," Milucrah said while assessing his wound. After a few days in her hands, his wounds had healed, and he was back with his comrades.

CHAPTER 68

Visits in the Night

I was extremely occupied with ruling the tribe. I began to engage more with Milucrah when she was available. We would discuss battle strategies or matters of spirituality. One night I invited her to my quarters. We drank cider and ate hazelnuts and walnuts, followed by blackberries and blueberries. We talked and talked in a manner we hadn't in a long time. After a time, we were reposing close to one another. I began to feel drowsy and slipped into a deep slumber.

Suddenly in my head I heard Estera calling out.

"Mordred, I wish to see you dear Mordred!" I wanted to answer her and also question her. Suddenly, I was conscious of her, standing in front of me naked.

"Estera, what happened to you?" I demanded. "Why did you disappear?"

"I never really disappeared, Mordred. I never left you and I am here now," she replied cryptically.

"I don't understand," I answered.

"What matters is the present. The past has irreversibly drifted away."

"But Estera, why are you here, now?" I asked her.

"We are two spirits that are going to be united by the power of the gods."

"But, Estera, I hardly know you. We spent one night together. It's true you enchanted me in a way few others have not managed to do, but still, it was just one night."

"Can we ever really know anybody, Mordred? You could spend a lifetime with somebody and still not really know them. We are all separate entities."

"You are wise and clever for one so young," I said.

"You want me to lie next to you, don't you Mordred?" Estera asked in a coaxing voice. She lay next to me and pressed her body next to mine. Suddenly I felt myself drifting away once again.

CHAPTER 69

A Second Visitation

When I became again conscious after a while, I became aware of another body, different from Estera 's slender one. Estera had once again disappeared to be replaced by another woman.

The woman had her back to me but turned to face me. It was the Iberian princess I had slept with.

"Mordred, why live in such a hovel?" said the princess critically. I felt aggrieved and mystified. What was this young woman doing in my abode?

"What are you doing here?" I demanded.

"That's no way to welcome me, now is it Mordred?" she replied with a little childlike giggle.

"You, princess, treated me like I was a freak. But I am not. I rule many tribes, I have acquired power and respect. You may live in your palace, but I am seen as a great warrior and leader."

"That you maybe, Mordred, but you are still a savage who holds on to obsolete beliefs and lives in what amounts to a shack." The princess's face was saddened.

"I have suffered, Mordred, since I last saw you. When Father heard what had happened by way of a loose tongued servant, that I had invited a savage to the palace and slept with him, he went into a terrible rage. He had me whipped and taken down to the basement, where I was thrown in with his dogs.

"During the long nights, I shivered with cold, and during the day I faced a long, solitary time. Father had ferociously argued with my mother and consequently, my mother and I were now strictly out of favour. His mistress and the daughter she had given him were now his favourites. Father had concocted a terrible fate for me. I was taken from the pen I shared with the dogs to my chambers. I was told to dress in my finest clothes, have a bath, put on make-up, and make myself as beautiful as possible. I began to jump to all the wrong conclusions. Perhaps Father and Mother had made up, or maybe Father's unyielding anger towards me had now relented.

I was placed on a large ceremonial throne and carried by four strong men out of my chambers. Soon, I was accosted by Father. His face clearly indicated he was still angry.

'Listen to me,' he ordered, 'tonight you will smile and keep your mouth shut. And if you don't, my daughter, I will have you whipped and taken to dogs I haven't fed for weeks, until they begin to devour you, my daughter. So tonight, don't utter a word and be fully compliant.'

I had no idea what he had in mind, but the menacing tone of his voice led me to believe he had a wicked plan and if I didn't acquiesce, an even more terrible fate awaited me. I had to wait a while before four strong men entered and carried me into the banqueting hall, accompanied by a fanfare played by the royal musicians, who only played during special occasions. There was a stir of surprise as the men in the room ogled me.

'You're selling your own daughter,' one man said before bursting into laughter.

'You must be really desperate,' said another.

'I present you, the Princess Aretaunin,' my Father bellowed.

I suddenly felt a sharp point in my back. Standing behind me, one of Father's men stood with a weapon he would prod further in my back if I did anything that might compromise my Father's devious intentions.

'Make your offers and make sure they are suitably large,' said my father.

A man with a large bag full of coins seemed eager to make a substantial bid. Most of the men were Father's age but some were considerably older. They had been invited to this sale only because of their buying power. Hands shot up and offers were made and quickly dismissed by Father.

Suddenly, the doors of the hall burst open, and a man walked in, followed by armed men. He was Father's biggest enemy, a war lord by the name of Ali Zanda.

The atmosphere had previously been jovial, but now a tension gripped the room.

'Why wasn't I invited?' demanded the warlord.

Father cowered, 'It was a mistake, an oversight. I offer my humble apologies.'

The warlord marched towards me and said, 'So this is the merchandise.'

I winced in fear.

The man was dressed in full armour. He had scars from various skirmishes, one that stretched across his cheek bone. He said eagerly, 'I'll take her off you.' His hands began to fondle me, then he yanked my mouth open and peered at my teeth. I wanted to scream, but the man standing behind me applied more pressure with the knife into my flesh. To add to my humiliation, he licked my face, bit me on the neck, then slapped me.

'You haven't paid for the goods yet,' said my father in protest.

'Don't forget the debt you owe me, Majesty,' replied the warlord. 'Here, take these coins.'

He casually flung some coins on the floor. Father looked sadly at the meagre amount of money.

'I think that should cover it,' said the warlord.

A man approached me, forcefully tied my wrists, and pulled me away screaming. Father was furious. He signalled to some of his men to do something about this effrontery, but none were prepared to take on the warlord and his men. I was dragged out of the palace to begin my life as a warlord's slave. The word slave seemed to repeat and repeat in my mind.

CHAPTER 70

The Next Visitors

When Princess Aretaunin disappeared, metamorphosing into, not one, but two people, the mother and daughter who had seduced me on the same night. I had never expected to see them again they were an old, distant chapter in my life.

"You never came back. You deserted us," the mother said in a pained voice.

"Yes, you abandoned us, and we were both with child," echoed the daughter in a sorrowful voice. Was I being confronted by all those I had done wrong, I wondered?

"I made a mistake, well two in fact. How was I to know? You came to me, what was I to do? Your problems are of your making," I tried to defend myself.

"Our lives have been a misery. We now live like slaves, like prostitutes. We are beholden to a wicked man, who now owns us, body, and soul. When we were forced to flee our family home, only Lasco Dracos showed us any kindness. He had no children of his own and his wife had recently died, as a great sickness raged through cities of our country.

"As we walked together, holding our infants, wondering where we would sleep, he beckoned to us and offered us refuge. He fed us and treated us with kindness. However, in time, he began to expect a reward for his generosity, and started whipping us and abusing us, making us do terrible things for his carnal pleasures. His cruelty knew no bounds."

The mother continued the story, relating more of the

misfortunes that had befallen them. I suppose I felt guilty, but my life had led me to other places, and I wasn't prepared at the time to be a father.

When the mother and daughter reached the end of their story, they hugged each other, gripping one another fiercely. And what of my offspring? Lasco Dracos had banished them, perhaps taking money from the sale. According to the mother and daughter, he was capable of all manner of evil.

The mother and daughter held each other until they slowly began to vanish, like disappearing shadows.

CHAPTER 71

An Odious Visitor

In time, I became conscious of a new being visiting me. I first became aware of its stinking, rank breath.

"Take me, Mordred," the being said in a crotchety voice. I was disturbed by this new arrival, lying next to me in my bed. I smelled more of its acrid breath, as its bony, long-nailed hands, as sharp as an eagle's talons, reached out to me. I recoiled, wrestling myself away.

"Leave me!" I shouted, feeling angry as well as being violated.

Suddenly, a thought occurred to me, a terrible unthinkable thought that filled my mind with horror. The being in my bed was the old hag I had seen many times before.

I managed to manoeuvre to the side of the bed and grabbed a dagger I had used many times in battle - a gift from a king I had helped defeat a neighbouring army. I yanked it behind my head and as I jabbed at the body of the hag, blood began to spurt out. I heard a shocked voice call out; it was Milucrah's.

"What are you doing, Mordred!"

Regardless, I kept violently jabbing, trying to snuff the life of this being I was sure was the odious hag. The bedding was soaked with blood, the hag ceased to move and there were no more voices. For good measure, I cut off its head.

I climbed out of the bed and vomited.

CHAPTER 72

The Realisation of What I Have Done Sets In

I let in some of the early morning light and screamed as I saw Milucrah's decapitated head and butchered body. Another terrible thought entered my head.

Milucrah was a priestess and had the power to transform into different beings. During the night she had been doing just that, shapeshifting, finally transforming into the hag.

My mind was in turmoil, I grabbed a few possessions, unsure where was I going and what I was going to do. I had no plans. I just ran out of the place I had always called home. I ran past the stream where I used to play with Milucrah. I hoped nobody would see me, or worse, chase me. My heart kept pounding and I was short of breath. The air was cold, great plumes of white condensation exiting from my mouth.

After a while, I could no longer run, so I walked at pace. Soon I reached unfamiliar surroundings. and heard the voices of approaching men, laughing. One of them was singing a lewd song. I quickly hid behind some bushes. They were members of a neighbouring tribe who would have slain me if they'd discovered me.

Crouching down, hardly daring to breathe, they walked by without noticing me. When I felt assured, they had gone far enough, I gingerly moved from my hiding place, my eyes darting about, looking for other dangers.

I lived on berries and scavenged for food. Once, I managed to trap a rabbit and ate it ravenously, having cooked it on a fire next to a small cave I had chanced upon. I never strayed too long in the same place. What if people were still looking for me?

Soon, I reached this great wilderness where I now dwell, a lost soul still grieving the loss of Milucrah, who died by my own hand. For I am a priest killer, bound to spend the rest of his days hunted and tormented. This until I enter Dubnos, the dark world that awaits me.

PART 4

CHAPTER 73

Killing Souls

It is the year 2042. A lot has happened in recent years. The world has dramatically changed, politically as well as ideologically. My name is Maz Zing. I am in my early thirties. I am a party official. To many, I don't exist and neither does the place where I work. My job is top-secret, highly classified.

I work for a correctional centre. Some, indeed, many, around the world would consider me to be a monster, who carries out the most despicable work. For me it is just a job. I perform the task of emptying minds of their previous religious notions and replacing them with the ideology of the Party.

In 2035, following the orders of the Party, practising religion having been banned, priests were rounded up in their thousands. Some came willingly, some were dragged away in fear. Some went into hiding, and the public was warned that they would be heavily punished if they were to give them shelter.

By order of the highest executive, they had been imprisoned. People had been shocked at the way they were being treated at first, but any sort of protest had been quickly and ruthlessly stamped out. A new section in Correction Camp 5071 had been set up, in a remote, desolate place, away from prying eyes.

And it was I, who was responsible for its smooth running. I had a whole team working with me, specially hand-picked guards - some of whom had a reputation for violence. I had received some basic training, but I also brought in my own ideas, which the executive seemed to approve of.

Upon arrival, the priests were told to disrobe. In turn they were handed a bright-orange shirt and bright-green trousers, which were chosen because they were totally at odds with their bland, black cassocks. The dormitories or cells they slept in were also painted in bright colours. Music blared out all day long, again totally different from the serious, sombre music they were used to. I insisted that there remained no links to their past lives. Their past had to be wiped out.

The first rule they had to learn was that no religious references were allowed. If this strict rule was broken, they would be put in solitary confinement and their food would be rationed to the bare minimum. If any two or indeed more were found together speaking, the punishment would immediately come into effect and their time in the correction camp would be extended.

They would also be called and addressed by others by a new name I deemed suitable. I enjoyed giving stern, flippant, ridiculous names they were forced to live with. My hope was that one day, they would eventually believe these were truly their names.

As a surname, I would sometimes give them an obscene word or perhaps sacrilegious one, such as Devillover, Christiansaliver, Bumtwit or Cockson. Their peers were forced to use these made-up names.

As you can see, the first part of their "stay" at the camp included a fair amount of humiliation. This phase also included a lot of counterindoctrination. Many of their key beliefs were said to be false, the objective being to rebut arcane theological arguments. We also showed them images of the suffering of those who had been victims in the name of "God". We would put forward arguments that the universe could have, and indeed did, emerge from nothing. We questioned the credibility of the belief in an all-knowing God and presented philosophical proofs against His existence. How could a god that pertains to being good, allow for a world so full of wickedness and evil? Surely, we argued, God as they envisioned Him would be able to prevent such evil.

We discussed all the religious ideas that are now obsolete, ever since cosmology had offered strong and more plausible theories. Every single point we made aimed to weaken the priest's resolve to hold onto their faith. We promoted the idea that we as individuals strive for success by our own ability, diligence and luck, not by way of religious mumbo-jumbo. Such ideas were repeated ad infinitum.

Often, we would mock Christ, and the utter absurdity of a crucified god and all the mythology created around him a couple of thousand years ago. Of course, they never had the chance to respond. Indeed, if they tried to, they were immediately, and severely, punished, before having to explain to their peers that they had made a grave mistake.

Adorned on the walls everywhere around the camp were large posters in bright, fluorescent colours with slogans such as "God doesn't exist and never did", "Priests peddle lies", or "Only party beliefs are true beliefs". Those judged to be irredeemably non-compliant were sent to the hospital wing, where their memories were erased through electroconvulsive shocks or drug-induced amnesia.

One day, it was brought to my attention that one of our most stringent rules had been violated. The culprit was an elderly man who wouldn't hurt a fly, totally harmless, and who had undoubtedly been a priest most of his life.

A warden searching through his room had discovered, hidden in his bed clothes, a small, home-made cross - two small pieces of wood and wire, left behind by the builders who had conducted repairs in the cells.

The warden, Zendon, marched the old man to my office.

"I found this cross, Madam Director."

Zendon held up the shoddy looking cross.

"Can you explain yourself, Comrade?"

Comrade Slop, as I'd named him, visibly shrunk but didn't reply at once.

Finally, he muttered, "It's a little comfort to prey to the Lord before I go to sleep. I mean no harm Madam Director."

"As you are well aware, Comrade Slop," I replied, my face stiffening, "such behaviour is totally prohibited. How long has this been going on?"

"Just a few weeks, Madam Director," Slop replied in a mournful voice.

"Are you the only one, or are there others?" I demanded, peering into his terror-stricken eyes.

"Only me, Madam Director, I can assure you."

"The thing is, Comrade Slop, you are setting a dangerous precedent. Others might follow your example," I said in a menacing voice.

"Yes, Madam Director," Slop said, tears welling up in his eyes, either because his "comfort" would be taken away from him, or because he anticipated I was about to administer a terrible punishment.

"Look at this, Comrade Slop," I said while taking out

of my drawer a beautiful, ceramic cross. Slop admired it, his eyes widening as if he was in rapture.

"Beautiful, isn't it Comrade Slop? Quite exquisite. Perhaps you know it, as it was on display in a cathedral for hundreds of years. Tourists always admired it, while believers prayed to it. Like you did with your pathetic creation of a cross."

Slop just stared at me, still fearful, wondering where I was going with this. "You did pray, to your God, didn't you Slop?"

"Yes, Madam Director," Slop answered like a contrite child.

"And, really, what purpose did this serve?" I asked, screwing my face up.

"To connect with the Lord, to ask for forgiveness, to have some kind of hope, Madam Director."

"The Lord won't come to your rescue, nor your God, Slop. Why? Because God doesn't exist, and the Lord is part of a mythology. People used to worship what they saw around them. First nature, then Christianity replaced these notions. Now science has disproved much of the concepts in Christianity." Comrade Slop didn't try to contradict me - he knew he would be punished.

I produced another object from the drawer. This time, it was a wooden cross with a glass compartment containing a morsel of wood. I looked at Slop, who by then was transfixed. I had checked his records, and knew he was an academic as well as an expert in religious artefacts. When he had been dragged from his home, he had begged that his personal collection of artefacts be spared. Of course, his wishes had not been granted. Any metals of value were melted. The church where he had been a priest for many years had been torn down and replaced with a Party building.

"You know what this is, don't you Slop?" I asked the former priest, who was staring at it in an adoring way. I was sure he would have wanted to hold it in his arms, to use it to worship, as he had done all those years as a priest.

"Yes, Madam Director, I have read about it, it is said it holds a part of the cross Jesus was crucified on."

"If you say so... But like most relics, it was probably cut from a tree by some fraudster, after which somebody made some outrageous claim that it came from the true cross., But I am sure you, Comrade Slop, wouldn't be so foolish and fall for such chicanery?"

Slop didn't respond. I went to a cupboard and brought out a 4.4 by 1.1 meters piece of cloth. I unrolled it on the floor. Slop gawped at it, in awe, hardly breathing, his eyes bulging, as if they might pop out of his head. I watched him attentively.

"You know what this is, Comrade Slop?" I asked, knowing full well he was perfectly aware of what it was. I just wanted him to say it out loud.

"The Shroud of Turin," he said, scrutinising it.

"Tell me more about it. To me, it looks like a giant rag that should be cut into strips and used to clean windows." Slop winced, and almost collapsed.

"Nobody in their right mind would do that," Slop said, shaking his head, shocked and tormented by my comment.

"But you will, tonight," I said in a deadpan voice, a half-smile on my face.

"No, no," Slop repeated, "this can't be true. I would never damage such a wonderful object with the Lord's face imprinted on it. It has been around for centuries. It is much venerated; it is one of the holiest of objects."

"Well, it is going to be disposed of and it will be

witnessed by the other priest while you, Comrade Slop, do it tonight. It will be quite a show. Comrade Slop, I'm sure of it."

I looked into Slop's desperate eyes; he was about to break down. These "holy" objects I had shown Slop, however, were fakes - the originals were still safely stashed away in the Vatican. There were copies of these relics in every correctional facility for priests, so that they would be tricked into thinking they were destroying the genuine articles.

Most of these fake relics had been pilfered from the Vatican. There were letters of great historical importance, such as the 1521 papal bull from Pope Leo X excommunicating Martin Luther, notes concerning the 1633 trial of Galileo, and even documents from the reign of Pius XI relating to deals made with Mussolini to protect the Church's interests.

There were maps and tapestries, not to mention statues and figurines. Apart from the Shroud, all the relics were from parts of the human anatomy. Bones and skin, dry, yellow-coloured fingernails, and even heads of saints were preserved, often bought and sold, sometimes stolen, but almost always cherished and revered.

There were some exotic relics, such as the dried blood of St Janarius, martyred in the 4th century AD, or the holy foreskin from Jesus Christ himself. There was the tongue of St Anthony of Padua, a great orator. The mummified body of Saint Mark. And the severed head of Saint John the Baptist. All these objects (fakes as I previously pointed out) were at my disposal to force Slop to destroy them once and forever.

Before the event, Slop was left alone in his cell to reflect on what he had to do. An announcement was made that all inmates were to assemble at eight o'clock in the grand hall, where instruction was given, meetings were held, and punishments were given.

The hall comprised a stage on which was a table holding fake but nonetheless authentic-looking religious artefacts. Next to the relics was a transparent vat of fluoroantimonic acid, the superacid powerful enough to eat through any object. Various apparatuses, hammers, drills, scissors, and spray canisters were also on show.

Cheesy organ music was playing to provide the background to the terrible show that was about to be performed, and bright spotlights everywhere to illuminate the stage.

The rabble of priests were gathering in the hall, whispering, speculating and fearful about what was about to take place. They all knew Slop to be a devout man, who often failed to hide his beliefs. Their sympathies lay with Slop, even those who had all but renounced their faith and were about to be released back in the world as they no longer constituted a danger.

Comrade Slop had been brought in by two guards, who had to drag him along as if he was about to be executed, rather than having to wantonly destroy objects.

There was a drum roll, and Slop could be heard yelling, "No, no, please no! I can't, I won't! I can't do this!"

His pleading eyes searched the room, as if demanding somebody come to his aid. Nobody did, of course - the guards were armed with batons, which they would use to prod and prompt anyone supporting the small, bony former priest.

Needless to say, I was there. Observing it all from a vantage point, dressed in a short skirt that showed off my long, tanned legs and a pristine, tight white shirt - a provocative outfit to these godly men.

"Let's get started, shall we, Comrade Slop?" I said in a smooth, enticing voice.

Slop stared at me, a look of horror in his eyes, a single tear meandering down his pale, veiny face. He was almost bald - just some well-cropped white hair on each side of his face - with contrasting bushy, slug-like eyebrows.

"No please! I won't make another cross, I will follow all the instructions, I will change my ways. I promise you, Madam Director, from the bottom of my heart."

"It's too late for that, the deed is done and now you have to prove you have put all your bad ways, behind you."

"No, please, I beg of you," Slop pleaded on his knees, in what seemed like a prayer.

"Beg as much as you like, Comrade Slop, it's not going to help. Now Mr Jinx, can you hand a hammer over to Comrade Slop please?"

Mr Jinx was a rather large man who struggled to get into his uniform. Feared by all the inmates, he could sometimes be pleasant, although more often than not he was just cruel - and sometimes violent. One of many guards to be avoided.

He ambled slowly over to Slop, having grabbed the hammer and shown it to the crowd who, out of obligation, had clapped and cheered, fearing they too would be punished if they didn't.

The ceramic cross I had showed to Slop earlier was on the table.

"Right, Comrade Slop, now smash the cross," I said in a soft voice, like a mother gently asking a child to do something. The words I'd just uttered flashed on a screen behind Slop.

"Smash it up."

The crowd were instructed to chant the words as they appeared on screen, to encourage Slop to complete the task.

"Smash it up. Smash it up, Smash it up." Some of the former priests had got into the vibe, having forgotten, it seemed, their holy ways.

Slop shook violently, his hands quivering. He took the hammer in his right hand, hardly able to hold it, as if it had been incredibly heavy - it wasn't, it was just an everyday, ordinary hammer to bang nails into walls. Slowly, he lifted it behind his head. The room held its breath.

"Now smash it," I said coolly.

Without looking at the object, he brought the hammer down, at the same time collapsing in a heap. Jinx walked towards him and lifted him back to his feet. Slop was ashen-faced, perspiration running down his face. He had all but missed the ceramic artefact. The hammer had connected with the tip, causing a small chip to be dislodged.

The word "again" flashed on the screen and soon the room was chanting "again, again, again". Slop was handed the hammer, which he slowly put behind his head. This time, he succeeded in smashing the artefact into small pieces. It was now worthless and meaningless, as useful as a broken teacup. "Good job, Comrade Slop," I said in a positive voice.

Slop couldn't bring himself to look at the damage he'd inflicted. However, the high-definition screen behind him showed, in slow motion, a clip of him bringing down the hammer, which sent pieces scattering all around him.

"Let's go for the wooden cross containing a piece of the real cross, shall we now, Comrade Slop?"

"No, not that! It would be a profanation. I would go to hell."

"Hell," I mocked, "you don't believe in that nonsense, do you Comrade Slop? Made up for children and simple folk to behave and keep in line."

Jinx prodded Slop with his baton, having handed him the cross-containing fragments from the real cross. A few steps and Slop was standing in front of the large vat of acid, transparent so that all could see what would happen when the cross was dropped into it.

Suddenly, the words "Drop it" flashed on the screen in large red letters. The crowd were now prompted to repeat the words as Lock, another guard, acted as cheerleader, encouraging them, shouting with great gusto.

Jinx prodded Slop a few times. Eventually, the former priest closed his eyes and released the cross into the vat of acid. It began to fizzle and in no time at all, it had disappeared – as if it had never existed.

The replay was shown a couple of times in slow motion on the high-definition screen.

"Good, Comrade Slop. Well done. You are getting the hang of things," I said softly. "What shall we go for next? How about the gruesome decapitated head, of, er what was his name… John the Baptist? What is the use of a head anyway? It's just clutter."

"But Madam Director, he is one of the most important people mentioned in the Bible. He baptized Christ himself," Slop spluttered.

"Well, now his head is going to be bathed in acid." I said sardonically.

"I won't do it," Slop said in a moment of pathetic

defiance.

"Oh, but you will," I replied calmly.

Jinx handed over the head, which was in fact a dummy's head wrapped in old, stained cloth - made to look old.

"I am holding the head of John the Baptist," Slop declared, his voice quivering, his whole body trembling.

He held the head above the vat, and with a scream released that, as he had done with the fragment of the real cross. And in the same way, the head fizzled and let off some smoke before disintegrating into nothingness.

Of course, the action was replayed a few times, in great detail and numerous angles, on the screen.

"You see, Comrade Slop, all these objects, are worthless and can easily be disposed of, without any sentiment. You have seen it for yourself now. They are only objects that hold value through superstition, ignorance, and lack of information," I said, smiling.

Slop didn't reply. He was catching his breath, trying to regain some composure. "Jinx," I called out, "get the cloth and put it on the floor. Comrade Slop has some work to do on it."

"No, not the shroud, not the holy shroud. It has Christ's face on it, the only true image we have of Christ."

"Now, Comrade Slop, don't get all silly. It's clearly a fake, created to make people believe it is the actual shroud in which your Jesus was buried and attract the masses to steal their money."

"You're lying," Slop said bitterly.

"Well, carbon dating revealed it was made during the Middle Ages rather than two thousand years ago. And just like many of these objects you worship, it's a fake."

The words "It's a fake" appeared on the screen. The

crowd began to chant while clapping - prompted to do so by the guard, Lock.

Slop was handed an aerosol can.

"Now write: It's a fake," I said in a gentle voice.

"Na, na, na, n, n, nn, no, no," Slop stuttered whilst being prodded in the ribs by Jinx,.

Reluctantly, he bent over and in scrawly, illegible writing, he sprayed the words "It's a fake". Again, the action was replayed on the screen.

Next, Slop was handed some large silver scissors.

"Now, Comrade Slop, I would like you to cut the cloth," I said warmly.

Even though the cloth was now defaced beyond repair, Slop was still reluctant to cut it. He gritted his teeth and closed his eyes, and began to cut the material, his image displayed on the screen.

"Keep cutting," I ordered, while Jinx occasionally prodded him. Soon, the so-called shroud looked like nothing more than a shredded rag.

"Let's put it in the acid bath, shall we?" I said, watching Slop, still snipping away. Jinx prodded him and Slop gathered it up in a ball. Gritting his teeth, he dropped it down the vat. It fizzed, smoked, and disintegrated in a split second.

I got Slop to destroy a few other "relics", a handwoven belt allegedly worn by the Virgin Mary, some holy breast milk kept in a small bottle, and Mary Magdalene's arm - minus two fingers after Saint Hugh had visited the Abbey of Fécamp and proceeded to bite off two fingers while the monks looked on in horror.

Added to this list was the head of Saint Catherine of Siena, who had once had a vision of Jesus giving her a wedding ring made of his own holy foreskin. Such was this woman's popularity when she died that the townsfolk of Siena wanted her whole body back to venerate. Which proved impossible, so they cut off her head instead and placed it in a sack.

For the finale, I couldn't resist the holy foreskin to be dropped in the vat of acid - the holy prepuce which gave Saint Bridget orgasms when bits of it were dropped on her tongue by an angel. Jinx casually handed the object - which was held in a glass canister with a golden top - to Slop as if it were a household utensil.

"Drop it down" appeared on the screen in large letters. Slop let out the scream of a wounded animal and dropped it. He collapsed to the floor, writhing in agony, as if he'd been shot in the stomach. Jinx and Lock grabbed an arm each and dragged him out of the room, still screaming. The audience went silent, whilst cheesy music once again filled the room.

"So Gentlemen," I said in a benign voice, "don't be making crosses any more. And stop believing in the power of these ridiculous objects which are just worthless and meaningless and have fooled people over centuries."

The crowd of priests had trooped out slowly, their morale undermined - which was part of the reason for this somewhat theatrical, absurd exercise devised by some sadistic party member, with some major adaptations from myself to give it a bit of zing.

The next day, I was in my office talking to a Party official when I heard a knock on the door.

"Come in," I called out, thinking nothing of it. Standing in the doorframe was Lock, a serious look on his face. I concluded my telephone call - there was nothing particularly important to discuss anyway.

"What happened?" I asked Lock, whose bent head

looked down at the floor.

"It's Comrade Slop. He's dead."

I was momentarily stunned.

"I would like to see the body," I said, still taking the news in. There had been a few deaths since I had been appointed. It was to be expected, as most of the men were old. This, however, seemed different, being the day after I had put Slop through a terrible ordeal. But I was trained to be cold and professional, and so I calmly walked alongside Lock to the small room that had been Slop's cell.

I expected an anguished face but to my surprise, Slop, or Father Ajay as he had been known in the old world, looked peaceful - as if he'd finally found peace. There was even a hint of a smile on his face, as if he was happy to relinquish his life.

My job is not to physically kill priests. It is to drain away all their religious beliefs and replace them with the banal ideas of the Party.

But in truth, I am a priest killer. For if you take away their beliefs, what remains?

I hadn't killed Slop, but in another way, I had. For what purpose did his life serve now?

Yes, I can't deny, I am a priest killer.

ABOUT THE AUTHOR

Francis H Powell is, amongst other things, a poet and writer of both short stories and novels. His anthology of short stories "Flight of Destiny" was published in April 2015 by Savant Publishing. His second book, "Adventures of Death, Reincarnation and Annihilation", was published by Beacon Publishing in December 2019.

Born in 1961, in Reading, England, Francis he was educated at various schools, before going to Art Schools, to complete a degree in painting and an MA in printmaking. He lives in Paris, where he published four short stories in "Rat Mort", a magazine specialising in dark and surreal stories, as well a magazine called "Freakwave".

He has had short stories and poems published in various magazines and websites. Signing for Poe Girl Publishing, we hope he will establish himself as a respected and prolific writer.

Printed by Amazon Italia Logistica S.r.l.
Torrazza Piemonte (TO), Italy

59605771R00150